"'To my beloved son, Lyle, and to my dear Kelsa...'"

Kelsa's gasp was echoed by Lyle's mother and aunt as the Hetheringtons' lawyer continued. "'I leave jointly, and in equal portions, all my business interests, all my stocks and shares in the Hetherington Group, all my—'"

Pandemonium broke out.

"No!" Lyle was instantly on his feet. "This is preposterous! Outrageous!"

"Utterly scandalous!" Mrs. Hetherington was on her feet, too. "It can't be legal! I'll contest it," she declared venomously. "It's iniquitous that *that* woman should..."

That woman! With those two slighting words ringing in her ears, Kelsa made for the door.

The sudden grip on her arm threatened to cut off her circulation, and she looked up, startled, into a pair of burning gray eyes. "*Now* tell me there was nothing going on between you and my father!" Lyle snarled.

Jessica Steele first tried her hand at writing romance novels at her husband's encouragement two years after they were married. She fondly remembers the day her first novel was accepted for publication. "Peter mopped me up, and neither of us cooked that night," she recalls. "We went out to dinner." She and her husband live in a hundred-year-old cottage in Worcestershire, and they've traveled to many fascinating places—including China, Japan, Mexico and Denmark—that make wonderful settings for her books.

Books by Jessica Steele

HARLEQUIN ROMANCE

3126—A FIRST TIME FOR EVERYTHING
3156—FLIGHT OF DISCOVERY
3173—WITHOUT KNOWING WHY
3203—RUNAWAY FROM LOVE
3215—HIS WOMAN
3227—BAD NEIGHBOURS
3256—DESTINED TO MEET
3294—HUNGARIAN RHAPSODY

RELATIVE VALUES

Jessica Steele

Harlequin Books

TORONTO • NEW YORK • LONDON
AMSTERDAM • PARIS • SYDNEY • HAMBURG
STOCKHOLM • ATHENS • TOKYO • MILAN
MADRID • WARSAW • BUDAPEST • AUCKLAND

ISBN 0-373-03308-7

RELATIVE VALUES

This edition published by arrangement with Harlequin Enterprises B. V.

Printed in U.S.A.

CHAPTER ONE

KELSA got into her car, coaxed it into life, and steered it from its parking spot outside her flat, then drove it in the direction of the car repair service she used. She had only lived in London for three months, but already the mechanics at the garage were becoming well known to her. Rarely, or so it seemed just lately, did a week go by without the Ford Fiesta—admittedly an old model—making a visit to the garage.

In her heart of hearts Kelsa knew that the time had come when she should part company with the car. But it had been her parents' car, the family car, and somehow she just couldn't bear to part with it, not just yet. It had been a big step for her to come and work in London, and she felt she needed a small breathing space before she took another large step.

Up until three months ago she had lived in Drifton Edge, an average-sized village in Herefordshire where she had been born and brought up. It was a pleasant village, and she had been quite happy living there until two years ago, when both her parents had been killed in an accident while holidaying abroad.

She had been twenty then, and for the best part of a year had been stunned, and grieving, and trying to come to terms with the fact that the two people she had loved so much were gone, and that she was now totally alone in the world. An only child, she did not even have grandparents to turn to. For her father had been an orphan, and her mother's parents had produced her late in life, and had died some years ago.

Kelsa felt she had her friend Vonnie to thank for the nudge she had given her, which had resulted in her giving up her job in Herefordshire. She had been chief bridesmaid at Vonnie's wedding six months before, and had been helping her into her going-away outfit when some remark had been made about 'a new life', and Vonnie had turned to her and, serious for a moment, had asked, 'What about *your* life, Kelsa?'

'What ab...? Oh, I expect I'll go on working at Coopers, and——' Kelsa began with a smile, but Vonnie, her expression still serious, interrupted her.

'You're wasted there,' she stated bluntly, being employed by the same firm and more aware than most that her friend's abilities were in no way stretched. 'Come to that, you're wasted here in Drifton Edge too!'

'I've always lived in Drifton Edge!' Kelsa protested.

'*Exactly*!' Vonnie responded.

'Oh, I'm all right,' shrugged Kelsa. Now was not the time to confess to her friend that she had felt unsettled for some time, with some nebulous urge swamping her every now and again to do something more than, different from, what she was doing.

'I worry about you,' Vonnie said flatly.

'For heaven's sake!' Kelsa exclaimed, and, attempting to tease, 'The only person you should worry about is your husband.' But if she had expected her good friend to forget the topic under discussion by being reminded of her husband of a few hours, then Kelsa realised Vonnie was not to be sidetracked. For instead of her serious look being replaced by a gentle smiling one, she remained so grave that Kelsa found she was volunteering, 'So OK, I'll look in the paper tomorrow and see what's going on in the job market.'

'Today. Do it today,' urged Vonnie.

'If it's going to put a smile back on your face—today,' Kelsa promised, and went home after the wedding with that unsettled feeling with her again. Perhaps Vonnie was right and she *should* think in terms of finding a more challenging sort of job than the one she did at Coopers. She had a brain, hadn't she?

In fact, her form mistress at school had been insistent that she apply for a place at university—only her mother, with her rigid, if loving, ideas of how she should be brought up, had been totally against the idea of her going away from home to any university. Instead, and firmly supported by her husband, she had suggested that Kelsa should enrol at the local secretarial college. And Kelsa, for the first time wondering if perhaps there were money difficulties which would mean that supporting her for some years more would be something of a problem, stifled the quick stirrings of excitement at the thought of going to university, and put her name down for secretarial college.

Later she realised that there had been no particular money problem other than those usually got over in most households, but that her parents' wish to keep her at home was nothing more than an extension of their protective attitude. It was an attitude which encompassed a strong emphasis being placed on her moral welfare, to an extent that even her friends, both male and female, were strictly vetted. Not that Kelsa was unduly upset or felt in any way stifled by parental authority, for, as she loved them, she knew herself much loved in return.

She came out of her reverie as she steered her car on to the forecourt of the garage. But while she waited for the service manager, who was in deep and technical conversation with another customer, she fell to recalling how she had come to abandon Herefordshire in favour of London. True to her promise to Vonnie, she had checked the paper and had spotted one likely-looking vacancy locally, but had suddenly been taken by another local vacancy—several, in fact—for staff required at a branch of the Hetherington Group, the mammoth multi-national company. A firm that size, she instantly realised, must have quite a turnover in staff, but did she want to work for them?

It didn't take her long to appreciate that in a company as big as Hetheringtons, surely they must have some sort of job she could do which might be termed 'challenging'. Without more ado she wrote after the Hetheringtons job, in the nearby town, and subsequently was amazed how big business worked, for she was promptly offered a job—in the London branch!

'But—but I live here!' she exclaimed, having already outlined a little of her circumstances.

'But there's nothing special to keep you here, is there? And we'd most certainly help you find accommodation.'

Kelsa went home having said she would think about it. Which she did, for a long while. In fact, Vonnie was back from her honeymoon before Kelsa had given Hetheringtons an answer. Kelsa told her about the job offer when Vonnie stopped by her office on her first morning back.

'What have you got to lose?' was her reaction. 'You could rent your house while you go and give it a try, and if it doesn't work out, they'd grab at the chance to have you working back here again.'

Indeed, what had she to lose? Suddenly, after so much time spent in coming to her decision, Kelsa knew what she was going to do. She reached for a piece of paper and took up her pen. 'I'm honour bound to give a month's notice,' she said, and grinned at Vonnie's squeal of delight and small hug.

The next decision Kelsa made was not to rent out her home. Somehow she just couldn't face that. Perhaps later, if things worked out well in London, she would think about selling it. But for the moment she couldn't take to the idea of strangers living with the things her parents had loved and, in some cases, treasured.

'Miss Stevens!' The service manager coming over to her and patting the bonnet of her car brought her again away from her memories. The service manager, as she had rather feared he might, then began to go into technical detail of what precisely was wrong with her vehicle. Her eyes glazed over.

'But you *can* fix it?' she butted in when he paused for breath. 'And I *can* collect it this evening?'

'I can fix it all right,' he replied, but, shaking his head, 'It won't be ready before tomorrow. January's a busy month, you see.'

Kelsa didn't quite see, though she suspected he must mean that poor weather conditions brought on a spate of car accidents. Her parents had died in a car accident, and she quickly turned her thoughts away from such things. 'I'll collect it tomorrow, then,' she said, and, handing over her car keys, went quickly from the garage.

Realising that she would have to take the bus home to her small flat that night, she headed for Hetheringtons, which fortunately was within walking distance of the garage. Fortunately too, the flat, which without the help of Hetheringtons she had found for herself, was unfurnished, and she had furnished it with furniture from her old home.

The Hetherington building hove into view, and a smile touched her mouth. With a warm glow she thought of how well—how surprisingly well, really—she had progressed since her first day at Hetheringtons, almost three months ago now.

Not that she'd done so well to start with. For to begin with she had dallied too long in accepting the original position she had been offered, so that the job was no longer open. But since she had burnt her boats, so to speak, in giving in her notice, pride had prevented her from rescinding it, and she had thought herself fortunate to be offered a further-down-the-scale secretarial job, to Ian Collins in the transport section of head office. Without hesitation she had accepted it.

The work, however, had been no more stimulating than the job she had held at Coopers. But then, however, when she had been working for Ian Collins for two months, something had happened which had dramatically changed that situation. Kelsa fairly bounced up the steps of the Hetherington building—and went in an entirely different direction from the transport section! She felt good inside as she recalled her fateful meeting one day with the chairman of the whole company.

Well, perhaps it wasn't actually a meeting, but more of a bumping into. For she had been on her way to another department on some errand when she had seen a tall, white-haired man of about sixty coming towards her. There had been no one else about at the time, but as she had neared him he looked across at her as if to briefly acknowledge one of his workers, when he had seemed to stumble and sway towards her.

In an instant, regardless that the air he had about him, the very cut of his suit, stated that he must be some top-floor executive, she had caught a swift and steadying hold of his arm. 'Are you all right?' she enquired swiftly, her voice gentle, musical as her mother's had been, as she stared at him in concern from frank, startlingly blue eyes.

'You're—new here?' he asked, taking his gaze from her as he straightened and took a step back.

Kelsa let go her supporting hold on his arm, though since he still seemed a little off colour, she stayed close. 'I've been here two months,' she smiled, delaying when she might have taken a step on her way, just in case he wasn't feeling quite as well as he was trying to appear. Regardless of who he was, she couldn't leave the man when he might be on the point of collapse. 'I work in the transport section—for Ian Collins,' she added, while her eyes assessed that he seemed to be quite shaken by his stumble.

'That explains why I haven't seen you about the place—I'd have remembered that smile,' he commented, quite gallantly, she thought. Considering the many hundreds of employees who must float around the corridors from time to time, in her view it would be a miracle if he could recall the face and the smile of everyone he came across. She was just thinking that she could safely leave him and go about her own business, though, when, watching her intently, he informed her, 'I'm Garwood Hetherington, by the way.'

'Oh!' she murmured, unsure what reaction he was expecting to that piece of information. But she had already guessed he must be fairly high up the Hetherington tree, so it wasn't too much of a shock to know that not only was he high up but that he sat on the top of the tree. 'The chairman,' she murmured, and instinctively, and because it just seemed right, she held out her hand.

'And you are?' he queried, shaking her hand.

'Kelsa Stevens,' she smiled, and realised that Mr Hetherington was every bit as busy as a chairman should be when, with a jerky movement that was almost a start, he looked abruptly away from her and checked the time on his watch.

'That's an unusual name,' he remarked, and, with a hint of a smile coming to his mouth as he looked at her, 'Have you any others?'

Feeling strangely at ease with the man, Kelsa felt none of the awkwardness she might have expected to experience. 'For my sins, my parents inflicted me with the label of Kelsa Primrose March Stevens,' she trotted out. Lest he should find her names funny, though, she looked away from him and braced herself under the pretext of consulting her own watch.

But there was no humour at all in his tone when, after a moment or two, he commented, 'One can only take it from that that you were born in March.'

She turned her glance back to him, feeling that same ease with him again. 'Early December, actually,' she smiled. 'My mother's name was March. I rather think that since she only had the one name she was over-compensating by giving me three, but...'

'Was?' Garwood Hetherington cut in.

'My parents were killed in a car accident two years ago,' she answered quietly.

'I'm—sorry,' he said gruffly, and, clearly a very busy man, without another word he nodded briefly and went on his way.

Over the next few days, the fact that the chairman of Hetheringtons had shown himself not too high-powered to pass the time of day with one of his employees began to fade from Kelsa's mind. Within the week, however, when the work she was doing had become so monotonous as to make her think of looking for another job, she had proof that the chairman had not forgotten her. And she could only be grateful then that, thanks to her name, which he seemed to think was unusual, he had remembered her when his PA had complained that he was giving her enough work for two.

She hardly dared to believe her luck when she received a request to go straight away to the chairman's office to be interviewed for the assistant to his PA's job. But, pushing a strand of her long blonde hair back from her cheek, she wasted no more time than that.

She took to Nadine Anderson straight away, and was pleased that the slender, well turned out woman seemed to take to her too. The chairman's PA was about forty, Kelsa thought, and interviewed her most pleasantly. But even so, Kelsa could hardly believe it when within a very short while she declared—despite all the others she must have interviewed—that she thought they would be able to work very well together.

With such speed that Kelsa was having a job taking it in, she had bidden goodbye to the transport section, and was in a matter of hours established at a desk in Nadine Anderson's office, and was already at work.

She learned a lot over the next three weeks. She had a quick and agile mind and soaked knowledge up like a sponge, and in no time was realising that she had never felt happier. The work, though strange at first, was within her capabilities, enjoyable, and kept her fully absorbed. There was a bonus, too, in that both Nadine Anderson and Mr Garwood Hetherington were always unfailingly polite and pleasant, no matter what stresses and strains went on around them. Indeed, as one week passed and then two, Kelsa realised she had formed an empathy not only with Nadine but with the chairman too.

On the personal side, Nadine, she had learned, was divorced but was newly engaged, though she was in no hurry to rush into a second marriage. Of the chairman Kelsa had learned that he was married and lived with his wife Edwina in Surrey.

Their son, Carlyle Hetherington, as well as being managing director of the Hetherington Group, was forward-thinking and took responsibility for new projects. Because Carlyle Hetherington—or Lyle, as his father affectionately referred to him—had been visiting their plant in Australia for the past month, Kelsa had not yet made his acquaintance.

But, as the lift stopped at her floor and she made a mental note to check the bus timetable for her return home that night, she realised that not only had she been working on the top floor for three weeks now, but that this week she might meet the Hetherington son and heir. He was due back either today or tomorrow anyhow, she recalled, and since according to Nadine he looked in on his father's office on average about once a week, then no doubt he would look in this week too. Lyle Hetherington, by the sound of it, was one of the world's achievers.

'I had ambition by the bucketload when I was his age,' Garwood Hetherington confided quietly one day when, again in confidence, he was telling her of his son's determination to find the hefty finance required for some diversification project he wanted started within the next two years. 'He'll get the backing he needs too,' he said proudly. 'Though how, with more than half the board against it, I'm having the greatest difficulty in seeing. But he's capable of being ruthless if he has to be, so it will be interesting to watch how things develop,' he ended admiringly.

Kelsa went into her office musing that she supposed one had to be tough to a certain extent in business, but hoping that the son, as well as being ruthless, had inherited some of his father's charm. Then she forgot all about him, because she could see that her employer had already arrived and had his connecting door open. 'Good morning, Mr Hetherington,' she smiled.

'Morning, Kelsa,' he responded, and, referring to the fact that Nadine, now confident that her assistant could cope, was having a few well-earned days off, 'Just you and me today, I believe.' With that the week got under way and in no time they were both hard at work.

It was gone eleven-thirty before Kelsa came up for air to realise that neither of them had thought of coffee. 'Coffee?' she asked the chairman, more aware than most of how hard he worked and thinking that at his age it wouldn't hurt him to slow down a bit.

'You're an angel!' he accepted, and a few minutes later laid down his pen to chat briefly to her.

Over the past weeks she had, bit by bit, disclosed a little about herself, including the fact that she had recently moved to London from Herefordshire, but that she returned to Drifton Edge most weekends during these winter months to check for burst pipes and the like.

In turn, she had pieced together from a comment he had made here and there that he seemed to enjoy work more than he enjoyed a home life. Though that in no way diminished the love and pride he had in his son, she realised. The son, a bachelor and very much enjoying his bachelor freedom, apparently, did not live at home but had his own property in Berkshire.

'Well, Kelsa,' the chairman smiled, 'you've been with me three weeks now. Do you think you're going to like it?'

'I love it,' she told him honestly, happily, and was again aware of an empathy between them.

'And your private life—you're not lonely in the big city?' he asked, and it seemed to her that he really cared.

'Not at all,' she assured him promptly. She had endless opportunities to go out on dates—it was her fault, not anyone else's, that, possibly on account of the strictures of her upbringing, she just wouldn't date all and sundry at Hetheringtons when asked.

'Good,' he smiled, 'I shouldn't like to think of you being unhappy.' He was so sweet, she thought, and realised that in a short space of time she had grown very fond of him. Then he took her thoughts away from that subject to enquire, 'How's that car of yours behaving?'

'That reminds me, I must find out the times of the buses tonight,' said Kelsa.

'Your car's in the garage again?'

'Overnight this time,' she answered, and smiled as she added, 'I'm going to have to think of changing it for something more reliable soon.'

'Well, don't worry about catching a bus tonight, I'll give you a lift home.'

'Oh, I wouldn't want to put you to any trouble,' she protested swiftly, and went on, 'Isn't your son arriving back today? You'll want...'

'It's no trouble to drop you off where you live, I promise you,' Garwood Hetherington assured her. 'As for Lyle, it's not certain he'll be back today—and if he is, if I know anything at all about him, he'll be so busy he won't have a minute to breathe!' He paused and, the matter settled as far as he was concerned, smiled, 'Shall we get on?'

At three o'clock that day Kelsa reminded her employer that he should be at his usual Monday afternoon meeting. 'They'll be waiting for you, Mr Hetherington,' she suggested.

'No, they won't,' he said lightly. 'Both Kendall and Pettit have gone down with 'flu, and Ramsey Ford wasn't looking too chipper when I saw him at lunchtime. I've put back the Monday meeting to Thursday. Which means,' he said as the idea came to him, 'that we can slope off early—how does that sound?'

Kelsa thought of the amount of work she still had to get through. But when she weighed that against her earlier thought that Mr Hetherington should slow down a little, she decided she could work twice as hard tomorrow.

'Sounds the best idea I've heard all week!' she laughed.

It was half past four, however, before they left the office, and Kelsa felt quite conspiratorial as they sailed down in the lift and then headed for the plate-glass outer doors. Nor could she help seeing that her employer, who was after all head of the whole combine, must be so unused to going home early that he really appeared quite guilty about it. He must have glimpsed the humour in her look as he held the door open for her, though, because, in another moment of empathy, they both laughed as they went out into the January night.

He was a nice man, and she felt comfortable with him as, giving him directions as they went, she answered any comment he cared to make. He had pulled up outside her flat, though, when suddenly he exclaimed, 'I must be slipping—there's an important phone call I meant to make!'

'Would you like to make your call from my flat?' Kelsa volunteered at once.

'May I?' he asked, and, making some comment to the effect that he must consider getting himself a car phone, without more ado he went with her inside the old building where she lived and which had been converted into flats.

'The phone's there,' she smiled, and left him to make his call in private while she went to take off her coat and scarf.

He had finished his call when, having given him an extra minute or two of privacy, she went back to her sitting-room. 'What a very pleasant room,' he commented, his eyes taking in her furnishings.

'The furniture came from my old home—it belonged to my parents,' Kelsa told him.

'Your parents were Herefordshire people too?'

'My father was,' she replied. 'My mother was born in Inchborough—it's a town in Warwickshire.'

'And you loved them,' he said gently, perhaps having heard something of the sort in her voice.

'We were a very happy family,' she smiled.

'I'm glad,' he said simply, and seemed about to take his leave when he remarked, 'You've no pictures of your parents on show,' and on impulse Kelsa went over to the small writing desk and took out a snapshot of her parents.

'This was taken a few months before they died,' she revealed as she handed the snapshot to him.

For some long seconds she stood by while, in silence, Garwood Hetherington studied the picture in his hands. Then, without making any comment about her father, he said softly, 'Your mother was very beautiful.'

'She was,' Kelsa agreed.

'And you,' he remarked in that soft tone, as though afraid of bruising her feelings if she still suffered from losing her only family, 'are exactly like her.'

That wasn't strictly true, in as much as Kelsa, while inheriting her mother's features, had hair that was more blonde than her mother's had been. Though while the stunning and beautiful blue of her mother's eyes did not truly come through in the photograph, it was a fact that Kelsa's eyes were that same striking and beautiful blue.

'Thank you,' she said anyhow.

'Thank *you*, my dear,' he replied. 'Thank you for showing me this picture,' and, handing it back to her, he turned and headed for the door. 'See you tomorrow,' he said lightly, and was gone before she could thank him for giving her a lift home.

He was the same friendly smiling man when Kelsa went into his office the next day. In fact, his smile had never seemed brighter, so that Kelsa just had to guess, 'Your son's home?'

He nodded, his smile becoming a grin. 'We haven't had a chance for much of a chat yet, but yes, he's home. I want to introduce the two of you the first opportunity I get.'

Kelsa got out some work, thinking that was a very nice thing for her employer to have said. Later, though, after she had met Carlyle Hetherington, she was not so sure how she felt. For it was mid-afternoon when, hearing a small 'Ouch!' followed by a minor oath from the next office, she looked in to see Garwood Hetherington trying to take a splinter out of his finger.

'You'd think that a desk that wears the badge of being an "antique" would have had all its rough edges worn smooth by now,' he complained, and seemed so much just like a little boy that, while Kelsa went forward to inspect the damage and then to remove the protruding splinter, she had to laugh.

It was at that moment, though, that as the music of her laughter faded some sound behind her caused her to half turn. And at once, as she observed that someone else had come into Garwood Hetherington's office, and looked at the dark-haired stranger in his mid-thirties, her whole being seemed to quiver with shock. Not that there was anything untoward in the man's appearance—if anything, with his straight nose and firm chin, he was quite good-looking. He was tall, taller than his father—for there was no doubt in her mind who he was. The trace of laughter was still curving her lovely mouth as her startlingly blue eyes met his—yet as her glance connected with the icy blast in the steel-grey of his eyes, Kelsa knew in that instant that this man was her enemy!

Her mouth fell open a little way from the shock of it. Why he should be her enemy she didn't have time to consider, because her pride was suddenly demanding that, even before they were introduced, he should know that whether he liked her or hated her on sight made no odds to her.

'Lyle!' his father exclaimed, all smiles. Turning to her, he went on, 'You don't know Kelsa, do you?'

'That pleasure has been denied me,' Lyle Hetherington murmured suavely, and Kelsa knew something else too—Lyle Hetherington was clever. Dislike her very much on sight he might do, but for the moment he wasn't ready to declare war.

Somehow, with Garwood Hetherington smiling fondly at the two of them, she forced herself to shake hands with his son. But to shake hands with him wasn't instinctive, the way it had been with his father, and Lyle Hetherington, for all his grip was firm—tinglingly so, almost—didn't make a meal of shaking her hand but let go of it as if having contact with her skin annoyed him.

'I wanted to have a word with you about our Dundee branch,' he addressed his father, his voice deep-timbred, his words cutting her out. Kelsa took the hint and crossed to the door. Casually, Lyle Hetherington strolled to the door too, and as she crossed the doorway he closed it, shutting her out.

Well! she thought, and, flabbergasted, collapsed on to her chair. She picked up her pen, but for quite some minutes was unable to concentrate on work. Had she imagined Lyle Hetherington's hostility? Had she imagined the ice glinting in his steely look? Had she imagined, been fanciful that before too long he would he declaring war on her?

Making an effort, she pulled some work in front of her. But, probably because she had never before met anyone who had taken such an instant dislike to her, she hoped she had got it all wrong. When some ten minutes later the communicating door opened, however, and Lyle Hetherington came striding out and with his eyes on her looked straight through her, and then strode straight on by without a word, she knew she hadn't got it wrong.

She spent the rest of the morning trying to concentrate on her work, while at the same time thoughts of Lyle Hetherington seemed to fill her head. His father had said he could be ruthless—but why on earth should she think he might be ruthless to her? Why would he bother? He was already managing director and in line for the job of chairman whenever his father chose to retire, so Nadine had said, so was it likely that a man who would one day run such an empire as the Hetherington Group would waste his valuable time on an assistant to an assistant to his father?

Kelsa had proof that indeed he would when that very afternoon, soon after Garwood Hetherington had left the office for the day to keep an appointment with Messrs Burton and Bowett, the company's solicitors, the outer door opened and Lyle Hetherington came in.

One glance at his icy expression as, with some deliberation, he closed the door to the rest of the workforce was all she needed to know that dislike hadn't changed to liking in the hours since she had last seen him.

However, rather than meet what looked like open warfare halfway, she began, 'I'm afraid Mr Hetherington has left early for an appointment. It's unlikely he'll return to the——'

'I know that!' Lyle Hetherington chopped her off before she could blink. 'It's you I've come to see.'

Kelsa most definitely did not like his tone, but being by nature fairly even-tempered, she enquired as steadily as she could, 'You wanted to see me about something?'—and was absolutely astounded at his reply!

'Just what the hell's going on between you and my father?' he barked furiously.

'What?' she gasped, and stared at him open-mouthed, certain she couldn't have heard him correctly. But from his grim expression, the ruthless forward thrust of his chin, she could see that Lyle Hetherington had no intention of repeating himself. Which left it to her to struggle free from her amazement, and to question, 'What in heaven's name do you mean?'

'The obvious, surely,' he grated, his tough look hardening. Clearly he was not giving a moment's credence to her shaken look. 'It's plain that something's going on between the two of you, without me seeing for myself the way you hold hands with him at every opportunity—laugh with him at——'

'Hold hands with him!' exclaimed Kelsa, the temper she rarely lost coming near to erupting—even though she still fought hard to keep calm. He must have witnessed her touching his father's hand, she realised, either during or after the process of her removing that splinter this morning. 'You've got it all wrong,' she lost no time in telling him, and went on to explain, 'If you'd come into Mr Hetherington's office thirty seconds earlier than you did, you'd have seen me extracting a splinter from his h...'

'Oh, for... Spare me!' Lyle Hetherington cut in toughly. 'Do I look as if I came down in the last shower?'

Most certainly he didn't. This man was tough, sophisticated and, she realised, somebody would have to be up very early in the morning to put one over on him. But she wasn't trying to put one over on him, so that all she could do was to protest, 'It's the truth! I swear...'

'You can swear as much as you like, Miss Stevens,' he started to fracture her calm by again cutting her off, 'but apart from my father barely waiting for you to leave his office this morning before telling me he'd got something of a "personal nature" to discuss with me...'

'It's got nothing to do with me whatever...' she attempted to cut him off this time, her voice starting to rise.

'Something,' he went straight on as if she had not spoken, 'which was so personal that he didn't want to discuss it with me here at the office—nor in his home,' he broke off, his voice grimmer than ever, 'where there's a risk that my mother—his wife of the last forty years—might overhear it.'

'I'm telling you it's got *nothing* to do with me!' Kelsa insisted emphatically. 'Whatever it is, it must be something connected with something else. I repeat, there is absolutely nothing going on between your father and me, and I...'

'You're not even fond of him?' he questioned jeeringly, adding cynically, 'Though, of course, you don't have to be.'

'I *am* fond of him. He's a super man!' she retorted hotly. 'But that doesn't mean that I'm having an affair with him or whatever it is you're implying. Grief...'

'Oh, I'm not merely implying it, Miss Stevens,' he snarled, 'I'm stating it. I've the evidence of my own eyes. Evidence of seeing you giggling like a couple of schoolkids yesterday when, not bothering to wait for five o'clock, he broke with tradition and left work early, to drive you to your home to be more *private* than the two of you were here.'

At that her temper broke. 'Don't be disgusting!' she flew, her brilliantly blue eyes flashing fire.

'You deny that you went in his car with him to——'

'No, I don't deny it! He was giving me a lift. We did leave work early, yes. But the only reason your father drove me to my home was that my car was in the garage for repair and——'

'My stars, and I thought I could think on my feet!'

'Will you stop interrupting me?' she yelled.

'Why the hell should I? I saw for myself the way you both tripped merrily from his car and into your flat—how's that for merely giving you a lift?'

So surprised was she by his statement that she actually blinked. 'You saw us?' she questioned, and, as her intelligence told her more than that, 'You *followed* us?' she asked, not quite believing any of this.

Lyle Hetherington smiled, a grim humourless smile. 'That's stopped you in your lying tracks, hasn't it? Yes, I saw you, yes, I followed you, and yes, I have perfect vision.'

'You're wrong—very wrong! Your father came with me into my flat, yes, but——'

'I don't need this!' he cut her off. 'I don't need any more of your lying invention, quick though your thinking powers might be. Your rise to this office from the typing pool in the short time you've been here has been meteoric.'

Typing pool! Anger like nothing she had ever experienced before rocketed up in her at his cool insolence. Clearly he had had her checked out and, just as clearly, he knew she'd been a secretary before her promotion. 'I'm a trained secretary,' she retorted heatedly, and, her fury too much to be sustained while sitting down, she slammed to her feet. 'And what's more, I'm a damned fine secretary—and good at my job!' she hurled at him.

To her further fury, he didn't turn a hair, but with his icy grey eyes on her furiously sparking blue ones, 'Make the most of it,' he gritted, his tone arctic. 'You won't be doing it for very much longer if I have anything to do with it!' And, having given her that to think about, Lyle Hetherington favoured her with a cutting look, and strode out.

Kelsa felt her chair beneath her without realising she had slumped down on to it. Feeling winded, she sat there for an age, barely able to credit what had just taken place.

For how long she sat stunned and staring into space, staggered and incredulous, she had no idea. But, by the time she had gathered some of her scattered wits and had left her desk to walk to the garage to collect her car, she knew that her confrontation with Lyle Hetherington had been no figment of her imagination.

Bluntly, that man had accused her of having an affair with his father! She could still barely take it in. Though as she drove her car home some fifteen minutes later she recalled once wondering if Lyle Hetherington had any of his father's charm. *Charm*! That *pig* of a man was totally devoid of it. The disbelieving swine—he was charmless to the core!

CHAPTER TWO

THOUGHTS of Lyle Hetherington, most of them furious, haunted Kelsa for most of the night. Her rise from the *typing pool*! The insolent, arrogant hound! And typing pool or no, how *dared* he intimate that she had been promoted via the bedroom?

Her fury cooled somewhat when fairness told her that, in all honesty, she couldn't say she had been promoted to the top floor because of her own efforts since she had been employed by Hetheringtons. She'd hardly been there long enough to make any sort of a mark, had she? And it was fair to say that there was small opportunity to show one's full ability in the transport section. Which left her having to acknowledge, as she had anyway, that were it not for Mr Garwood Hetherington's having a slight stumble that day, and stopping to chat for a brief while, and from that episode remembering her name, she would never have been among the interviewees, nor secured the promotion she had.

But that was still miles away from anything as sordid as Lyle Hetherington had dared to suggest. She was very fond of his father, but there was no harm in that. He liked her too, she knew it, but that was as far as it went. He was, as she'd told his ghastly son, a super man. He was always friendly and courteous and... Grief! Why should she have to defend what up until then had never needed defending?

Kelsa got up, bathed, dressed and had a bite to eat, then drove to work, once more fuming at Lyle Hetherington's outrageous remarks. While she admitted that she might have taken a short cut to promotion, she had, she knew without conceit, acquitted herself well in her new job, and at the end of the day had proved herself worthy of that promotion.

She walked into the Hetherington building knowing that while it was true that Nadine, at her interview, hadn't exactly given her the third degree, since Nadine was as sharp-minded as they came, and since she had needed help, not hindrance, she wouldn't have stood a chance of being offered the job if in Nadine's estimation she wasn't up to it.

Having got that satisfactorily established in her mind, Kelsa entered her office with her insides churned up at the thought that Garwood Hetherington might have had his discussion with his son that was of a 'personal nature' and that his son might then have gone on to accuse his father as he had accused her. She knew she would just cringe with embarrassment if her employer felt so badly that he felt he had to apologise for his son's allegations.

But it was clear to her straight away that, whatever it was Garwood Hetherington had discussed with his son, his son had not said a word to him of his suspicions—for he greeted her, 'Good morning, Kelsa,' and seemed on top of the world, with no hint whatsoever that he might be feeling in any way awkward or apologetic.

'Good morning, Mr Hetherington,' she returned with a relieved smile, and got down to work with her head still plagued with a problem which plainly, and to her relief, her employer knew nothing about.

Why, she wondered, when Lyle Hetherington, as he'd shown, was a man who went right to the heart of the matter, had he not tackled his father on the issue? He'd know by now, surely, from any 'personal' chat his father had had with him, that that personal matter had nothing to do with her. Though that still left Lyle Hetherington with the evidence he had—her rapid promotion, the hand-holding, his father going into her apartment building with her—believing that she and his father were up to their ears in an affair.

At that point Kelsa felt so sickened she almost went in and told Garwood Hetherington everything about what had happened after he had left the building yesterday. But she couldn't. How could she? Mr Hetherington thought the world of his son—not that anything she said would alter that in any way, but she didn't want to be the one to instigate any small rift, of no matter how brief a duration. Besides, her working relationship with her boss had been terrific. But if she did tell him, then if he realised she was embarrassed, Mr Hetherington too would be embarrassed, and surely that would create a strain, all previous ease of manner and empathy gone.

Kelsa went home that night having expected that at any moment Lyle Hetherington might roar in to 'confront' the two of them. She slept better that night, though, but went to work the next day glad that Nadine Anderson was back.

'Been busy?' Nadine enquired.

'You're joking!' Kelsa laughed. The turnover of work in their office was tremendous.

'Any problems?'

Kelsa felt dreadfully tempted to confide in Nadine, but somehow she couldn't do that either. 'Nothing I wasn't able to handle,' she replied—and spent her spare minutes wondering if she could have handled her encounter with Lyle Hetherington on Tuesday any better.

The day sped busily on, but while it was still at the back of her mind that he might yet come to his father's office at any moment to air his accusations, it was from Nadine that she learned she could relax on that score.

It was mid-afternoon, Garwood Hetherington out of his office and at a meeting, and they were having a few minutes' break with a cup of tea, when Nadine enquired if Kelsa had seen anything of Lyle Hetherington yet.

'He dropped in for some discussion with his father last Tuesday,' Kelsa answered carefully.

'And?'

'And?' queried Kelsa, and Nadine laughed.

'If you're not impressed, you're the only female in the building who isn't!'

'Impressed?'

'Come on, admit it. He's got it all, hasn't he?'

'As the saying goes,' Kelsa quipped, 'handsome is as handsome does.'

'And none do better than our Lyle,' Nadine smiled. 'Not that he dates anyone from here—he keeps his business and personal life strictly private.'

'No hope for me, then,' joked Kelsa thinking that, the way she felt about the odious creature she'd break a leg rather than go out with him—should he ever ask, which he wouldn't.

'Nor any of the local lovelies at the moment,' said Nadine, and at Kelsa's querying look, 'According to Ottilie, he's in Dundee for the rest of the week.'

'Oh,' Kelsa murmured, and actually felt the tension go out of her, and only then did she realise just how wound up she had been since Tuesday. 'He gets around, doesn't he?' she commented, aware that Ottilie Miller was the managing director's PA. 'When's he coming back, did Ottilie say?'

'For someone who's not interested . . .' teased Nadine, but supplied, 'Monday, I believe. Though I expect, as is normal when he gets his teeth into anything, he'll work over the weekend and fly down Monday or Tuesday.'

To show that she was no more interested than that, Kelsa got up and collected the teacups with the idle remark, 'He sounds like a busy man.'

Her own weekend was far less productive. She drove to Drifton Edge, but felt so unsettled that she returned on Sunday morning rather than in the afternoon, which was what she usually did. While she was feeling far less stewed up than she had been, she was still very much shaken by the interpretation Lyle Hetherington had placed on the perfectly innocent events he had witnessed.

He'd been furious, she recalled without the smallest effort. That fury was quite plainly all on account of the way he thought his father was deceiving his mother. Though since his father was the same lovely and pleasant man he had always been at the office, with nothing in any way strained in his manner, Kelsa was certain his son had not been in touch by phone from Scotland to state what he believed his father was up to with his PA's assistant.

But Kelsa started to feel quite furious herself again when she went to bed on Sunday night, and thought of the nerve of the man. How *dared* he! She was again inclined to tell his father, but again knew she couldn't. Although she recalled Lyle Hetherington's threat that she wouldn't have her job for very much longer, she couldn't see how he could get rid of her. Not, since she worked for his father, without first telling him why. In which case his father would put him straight in no uncertain fashion. All she hoped was that, when he saw how totally mistaken he had been, Lyle Hetherington would have the decency to apologise.

They were so frantically busy in the office on Monday that by lunchtime Nadine glanced across to Kelsa and commented pensively, 'I wonder what our chances are of having another assistant?'

'Where would we put her?' laughed Kelsa.

'You're right,' Nadine grinned, and got back to work again.

They had something of a respite when Garwood Hetherington went off to his usual Monday afternoon meeting, but only to find he was in a workish mood when he returned early. 'Anyone fancy doing a spot of overtime tonight?' he enquired cheerfully.

He was such a good boss there was little that Nadine or Kelsa would not do for him. 'Of course,' they chorused, and were still hard at it at half past seven.

A short while later, though, he came and stood in the doorway of his office. 'Dinner!' he announced. 'Who's ready for dinner?'

Garwood Hetherington had taken them to dinner once before when they'd worked late, and Kelsa had seen nothing wrong with that. But she had been very much affected by his son's vile insinuations, and this time, and solely on account of Lyle Hetherington, while hating him for making it so, she felt she had to wait for Nadine to confirm that it would be a threesome before she admitted that she was starving.

'Just watch the speed with which I get my coat on!' Nadine accepted the invitation, and in the rush to get to some food they were in Garwood Hetherington's car—the plan being that he would drive them back to the car park to pick up their own vehicles after he'd fed them—before either of them had stopped to wash their hands or comb their hair.

That was soon remedied, though, once they got to the smart restaurant and Kelsa and Nadine headed for the powder-room. 'Now, what will you have?' their host asked when they were reunited again and had been shown to a table.

But, 'My ring! My engagement ring!' Nadine exclaimed and, for the first time since Kelsa had known her, she looked a little flustered as she excused herself and anxiously headed back to the powder-room.

'So,' Garwood Hetherington laughed, 'what will *you* have, my dear?'

Kelsa took her eyes off the menu and looked at his face, alive with humour, and had to laugh too—he was such a dear man. As he looked down to concentrate his attention on his menu, however, her glance flicked away from him and over to the entrance to the dining-room. Then she froze in horror. She had been looking expecting to see Nadine returning to their table and who did she see but Lyle Hetherington! And he, clearly furious, had seen her!

Her stomach turned over as she saw him take an outraged step in their direction, as if then and there—and in front of the whole restaurant—he would come over and sort them both out. Desperately she prayed for Nadine to walk in, because it was patent that Lyle Hetherington thought she was dining *à deux* with his father. But of course Nadine did not appear.

Then suddenly Lyle Hetherington seemed to remember that he had a companion of his own. For, with such control that she could barely credit it, he had swiftly swung round and presented Kelsa with his back. And, while Kelsa's jaw was ready to hit the table, in the next moment he was escorting his gorgeous brunette dinner date out from Kelsa's vision.

She gaped after them; it had all happened so fast, she could barely take it in. She looked at Garwood Hetherington, but saw he was still deep in fish, meat or vegetarian choices and was entirely unaware that his son, his furious son, had in the space of a minute at the most been and gone.

It was all too obvious to Kelsa then that, swift in his decisions, Lyle Hetherington had changed his mind about having a row with his father in the restaurant. Though what he'd told his date as he'd turned her round when she must have been expecting to dine any moment, Kelsa couldn't begin to guess.

She was still feeling very much shaken by what had happened when Nadine, a smile on her face to denote that all was well, came back.

'You found it?'

'It was there where I left it,' she answered, and, as the three of them ordered, Kelsa wasn't too surprised that although ten minutes earlier she had been starving, she now no longer felt hungry.

Rather than cause comment, she did her best with her meal, but she had a sinking certainty inside that tomorrow, without fail, Lyle Hetherington would come storming into his father's office for a showdown. Had Nadine not been there Kelsa thought she might have found the courage to give her employer some hint. Which was ridiculous, she admitted in some confusion, for, had Nadine not been there, then she was fairly sure that she wouldn't be either. Because of his evil-minded son, she'd have made some excuse *not* to dine *à deux* with his father.

'Ready?' asked Nadine.

'Yes,' Kelsa smiled, vaguely aware that her employer and his PA had been discussing Lyle Hetherington's planning structure and how his father had proudly stated that he'd only spent Tuesday in the office since he'd got back, but already he had got Ramsey Ford, one of the directors, wavering. Garwood Hetherington, admiration for his son in every syllable, had gone on to endorse his view that despite the opposition he was getting from other quarters Lyle would most probably get the backing he required.

It went without saying, Kelsa realised as she sat with Nadine in her employer's car and he drove them back to the firm's car park, that Mr Hetherington, with his majority stockholding, would put the weight of the chairman's vote, his shares, behind his son if need be.

But as they pulled into the car park and all three of them got out of the car, she could not help but find it painful that, tomorrow when he had heard what his son had to say, he might not be so admiring of him.

Again she felt tempted, regardless of the embarrassment it would cause her, to give him some hint. But Nadine was there, and they would all end up embarrassed if she did. Besides, as they stood in the glow of a high lamp in the car park, Kelsa suddenly noticed how tired Mr Hetherington looked. Which wasn't surprising; he'd worked long and hard that day. She decided to leave him in peace. Tomorrow would come soon enough.

'That was a lovely meal, thank you.' She smiled prior to walking away to her car.

'Thank you, Kelsa, Nadine,' he replied, then confessed, with charm and humour, 'My wife flew off to join a winter cruise on Saturday—I didn't see why I should eat a solitary dinner!'

Kelsa drove home with her thoughts for her employer gentle as again she thought what a dear man he was. There was even a smile playing around her mouth as she thought of his humorous parting comment.

There was no smile on her face as she drove to work the next morning, however. Today—she knew it as she remembered Lyle Hetherington's expression of absolute fury last night—he would be presenting himself at his father's office to charge him with what he believed. Indeed, since Garwood Hetherington usually arrived at the office before either her or Nadine, and the son was as early to start work as his father, it wouldn't surprise her if the confrontation had already taken place.

Hating unpleasantness of any kind, and particularly when she realised she must be at the dead centre of this particular load of unpleasantness, she went into her office with her insides in a turmoil—and was met by a beaming boss.

'How's Kelsa?' he greeted her.

'Never better,' she smiled, and as Nadine came in close on her heels she turned to exchange greetings with her.

All that morning Kelsa felt on edge, just waiting for the door to open and for Lyle Hetherington to come striding in. But he didn't come, and Kelsa, still on edge, wished she could put the wretched man out of her head.

She wasn't hungry at lunchtime but went and bought a coffee and a sandwich in the staff canteen, while a new and startling worry suddenly presented itself. Did anyone else, all at once she paused to wonder, see the way she'd been promoted, the way she behaved with her employer, as more than it so innocently was?

Oh, heavens, she fretted, as she pushed her unwanted sandwich away from her—did they? Should she perhaps act differently towards him than she normally did? But grief why should she? She was only being natural, for goodness' sake! And surely Nadine, who as well as being a top-notch person to work with was plain-speaking enough, would have made some comment before now had she spotted anything she thought untoward. And anyhow—Kelsa started to lose some of her even temperament—Mr Hetherington was old enough to be her father! Her grandfather, come to that!

Suddenly she started to get angry. Why should she act differently? Garwood Hetherington's little quips amused her through the day, so why shouldn't she laugh if she wanted to? It was a pleasure to work for him, and—and his evil-minded son could go to hell or, if not there, back to Australia as soon as he liked—she wished he'd never left the place!

She was glad of her anger some five minutes later as she was going along one of the corridors in the building, when whom did she see coming towards her but Lyle Hetherington? He was tall, distinguished-looking and immaculately suited, and as her heart gave a lurch she knew he wouldn't deign to speak to her.

And that suited her fine. She was almost level with him when, angry enough to look through him for a change, she flicked a stony glance at his face. Oh, my word, she thought, and nearly quailed when, his arrogant icy look beating hers into a cocked hat, his steel-grey eyes pierced hers with such a look of malevolence that she knew she had chosen the wrong person to make an enemy of.

All she could do was tilt her head in the air another fraction or two, and to sail on by as though she was totally blind to that look that said he hadn't finished with her, not by a long way.

But her anger had gone and she was feeling quite shaken when she got back to her office. She spent the afternoon still expecting that Lyle Hetherington would stride in at any moment, and in fact she got so wound up at one point that she wouldn't have minded at all if he did come in to see his father. All his father had to do was to convince him of the truth, and it would all be over. Really, she thought, getting cross again, it was quite ridiculous!

But of Lyle Hetherington there was no sign that afternoon. And when at half-past four his father came and stopped by her desk and told her that as she'd worked late last night she could go home now if she liked, a certain stubbornness not to run off as though with her tail between her legs—not to mention her workload—made her refuse to leave early. 'No,' she said, and because it wasn't fair and she just was not going to let anybody dictate what her responses should be, she gave her employer a lovely smile and told him cheerfully, 'I like it here.'

His answer, after a brief moment of staring at her, was to stretch out a hand and, just as though she were a two-year-old, ruffle her hair. 'Beautiful child,' he commented, and seemed happy, Kelsa thought, as he went back to his office to wait for some paperwork which Nadine had left the office to sort out.

Kelsa remembered the way Garwood Hetherington had been with her as, changed into jeans and a shirt, she stood doing a few bits of washing about eight o'clock that night. Oh, how she wished his abominable son had been there! Had he seen the way his father was with her, the way he had referred to her as a child, then there would have been no doubt in his mind but that there was absolutely *nothing* going on between her and his parent.

She sighed at what seemed the inevitability of Lyle Hetherington taking up her thinking time. For it seemed that he had been there, had taken up permanent lodgings in her head, ever since she had first clapped eyes on him in his father's office last Tuesday.

Wondering why he hadn't entered his father's office at all *this* Tuesday occupied Kelsa for some while. But by the time her washing was spun dry and was hanging up in her kitchen to finish off, the best she could come up with was the memory of a woman she had worked with at Coopers. The woman's husband, she recalled, had been having an affair, but when confronted by his wife, had—to her sorrow and further unhappiness—instead of giving the woman up and toeing the line, left her to go and live with the other woman. Was that why, despite that malevolent look Lyle Hetherington had thrown her, he was not doing anything about it? Had he decided, being clearly more worldly than she would ever be, that his mother's best interests lay in him doing precisely nothing?

Kelsa made herself a cup of coffee and took it with her into her sitting-room, but she was still thinking of Lyle Hetherington when the doorbell rang. She went to answer the door—and could hardly believe it. For, not content with almost exclusively occupying her head, there in front of her, grim-expressioned and uncompromising, stood none other than Lyle Hetherington!

This was something she hadn't thought of: that he would take it into his head to call at her address! But, even if her heart was suddenly banging away like crazy as, taking his time, he let his icy grey eyes rake over her, Kelsa was not of a mind to let him walk all over her.

'Since you've obviously come here to see me, I suppose I'd better invite you in,' she opened belligerently. In she would invite him, but no way was she going to ask him to sit down. 'I trust this won't take long,' she added for insolent good measure as, closing the door behind him, he followed her into her neat and tidy sitting-room. This man owed her one very big apology, and suddenly she wanted that apology more than she'd ever wanted anything.

But so much for an apology, because Lyle Hetherington barely waited for her to stop and turn round to face him before enquiring nastily, 'Not seeing my father tonight?'

'Quite plainly you've not seen your father to acquaint him with your ridiculous notion that he and I are having some cheap affair!' Kelsa erupted, her anger on a much shorter fuse than she had thought.

'I doubt you come cheap, Miss Stevens,' he fired back insultingly. And for the first time in her life she understood why some women found that there were moments when they could cheerfully take a swipe at some man's head. Though she had more self-control than that, of course, but that didn't stop her from being angry, especially when, as if deliberately trying to goad her, 'Ridiculous notion, is it?' he questioned, but as she opened her mouth to speak, 'Do you deny that you were out dining with my father last night, that...'

'We'd been working late,' she got in quickly, but didn't have the chance to add that Nadine Anderson had been there too, and that he'd have seen her if he had waited around, though he wasn't the waiting-around sort.

As he again proved by riding harshly over anything she might have added to thunder, 'Women like you make me want to throw up!'

'Now just a...'

'He's about old enough to be your grandfather!'

'I know that!' she retorted, her voice starting to rise.

'But that still doesn't matter, does it?' he snarled.

'Of course it doesn't matter!' she flared. 'There's nothing *to* matter. I'm merely an assistant in his——'

'You sure as hell didn't earn your spurs the hard way! You...'

'If you're referring to the way I was promoted,' she butted in hotly, 'I know, I've realised, that it doesn't seem totally—er—above board. But I bumped into your father at work one day, and one thing led to another, and——'

'I'll say!' he sneered.

'And,' she stormed on, 'and he asked me my name, and because he thought it an unusual one, he remembered it when Nadine Anderson mentioned that she could do with some help.' There! She'd managed to get that cleared up.

Only Lyle Hetherington, his look tough, wasn't believing anything she said, not without first putting it under a microscope, she discovered—and not even then!

'And of course he doesn't find you attractive,' he taunted, as she paused for breath.

'I...'

'And of course he's never ever shown you any sign of—for the want of a better word—affection?'

'I...' she said again, and was about to say 'no' when she remembered the affectionate way Mr Hetherington had ruffled her hair that day. But then she didn't get the chance to say anything, because Lyle Hetherington had seen her hesitation, and, as his mouth firmed, he went straight into the attack again.

'Something holding back your lying tongue?' he charged abusively.

'No!' she protested. 'Your father likes me, I think, but...'

'Come now, Miss Stevens,' he mocked, 'surely you *know*.'

'Very well, then,' she flared, though she saw from the sudden narrowing of his eyes that he was expecting her confession to be something far more along the lines of his own thinking when instead she said, ignoring the sudden jutting of his chin, 'Yes, of course your father likes me, as I like him. But that's only normal, surely?'

'Your idea of what's normal and mine are very much at odds,' he advised her bluntly.

'Oh, look here!' she snapped, more than just a little fed up with him. 'Even you with your warped thinking must acknowledge that you'd never tolerate having to work with a PA—or PA's assistant, for that matter—whom you couldn't stand the sight of.'

'And my father likes the sight of you, doesn't he?' He refused to be sidetracked, though that had never been her aim.

'He...' she began, but she was the one who was sidetracked as she remembered how, in this very room, her boss had studied the snapshot of her mother and declared her beautiful, and had added that Kelsa was exactly like her. Today, too, he had said she was a beautiful child.

But she'd hesitated too long, and it didn't take the hard-eyed man in front of her a moment before going for her again. 'Warped mind,' he tossed at her. '*My* warped mind! When in this very flat you've entertained a man old enough to be...'

'He only stayed long enough to make a phone call he'd forgotten about,' she attempted, but she could see from the contemptuous way Lyle Hetherington was looking at her that he thought she was lying. And she'd never had anyone contemptuous of her before, and that not only hurt but sickened her. 'If you've anything else to add, put it in writing!' she exploded suddenly, and with her brilliantly blue eyes flashing fire she went to march round him on her way to show him out.

But she didn't get that far. For suddenly one of his hands snaked out and caught hold of her arm in a grip of iron, and, as if to let her know that he'd be the one to decide when this interview was over, he moved her until she was back standing in front of him again.

'Now what?' she stormed angrily, objecting most strongly to being manhandled by him or anybody else. 'Just why have you come here, Lyle Hetherington?' she yelled. 'You're not interested in listening to——'

'Forget me,' he cut her off, 'and let's get down to what *you're* interested in.'

'Me?' she queried, her brow wrinkling as she tried to get on to whatever wavelengths he was on now.

Icily his grey eyes pinned her, then to her utter stupefaction he told her, 'Since it's all too obvious that what you're interested in is the Hetherington money, I'm here to ask you, Miss Stevens, how much?'

So great was her shock that she didn't take in straight away what he was saying. Then, 'H-how—much?' she spluttered. 'You think I'm after your father's *money*!'

'Without question you are!' he rapped. 'Though, since you'll find that my money is every bit as good as his—how much will it cost *me*?'

'Cost *you*?' she gasped, some last thread of incredulity still not letting her believe he was saying what it seemed as though he was saying.

'To pay you to leave him alone,' he ruthlessly severed that last thread, his expression all arrogance. 'To leave him alone and...'

It was as far as he got. A red-hot mist suddenly clouded her vision, and *bang*! Kelsa hit that sneering arrogant face with all the strength at her command.

The sound of her violent slap on the side of his face was still ringing in the room when, his reaction equally explosive and immediate, 'Why, you...' he roared in outrage—and it was clear that no woman had ever hit him before. Nor, Kelsa swiftly realised as his hand again shot out and he held her, was she going to be allowed to get away with it.

Too late to put some distance between them, she was still standing there when, although if anything she would have thought he would have hit her back, instead he did nothing of the kind. But that hand was again as hard as iron round her arm, and he used it to pull her one-handedly up against him. In a flash Kelsa read what his intention was, and as his other arm came round her she had already begun to fight.

'Don't you dare!' she screeched, but discovered she was wasting her breath.

Then she didn't have any breath at all, for Lyle Hetherington had her locked in his arms, his head was coming down and, all in a moment, his mouth over hers.

'No!' she gasped for breath when he let her mouth free. But the freedom was only hers for a moment, because, as if he was hell-bent on teaching her a lesson she would never forget, Lyle Hetherington's mouth was there to claim hers again. 'Let *go* of me!' she screamed in panic the next time she had the chance, but again his lips were over hers and she made no more headway than before.

Valiantly she fought him, kicking and punching where she could, terrified suddenly when she felt his hands warm under her shirt, his hands roving where they would. She had taken her bra off to rinse through with the rest of her washing, but when those warm seeking fingers moved round to the front of her and captured the swollen globes of her breasts, she was more outraged than ever.

'Take your hands off me!' she shrieked, and with a dry sob of fear she pushed him with all her might—the result being, however, that she knocked the pair of them off balance, heading into her settee.

One good thing about that, though, was that Lyle Hetherington took his hands from her breasts, from beneath her shirt, as though to check that they would land without harm. But then, strangely, as she found she was lying, winded, beneath him on the settee, and staring up at him from wide distressed blue eyes, it was as though something of her real fear had communicated itself to him. For the next time he kissed her his lips were kind, and not bruising at all. His lips were gentle, giving, not taking, and all at once Kelsa was having difficulty in remembering what she had been so frightened of.

She closed her eyes, felt his kisses stray from her mouth to tenderly caress her throat. And suddenly then her thinking patterns went haywire, because something was happening to her that caused her not to want to fight him, but to welcome him.

Without thinking at all, but acting on instinct alone, her arms went round him. A sigh of pleasure broke from her as, once more he placed his superb mouth over hers.

'Lyle!' she breathed, and had never known anything as beautiful as the kiss they shared. His kiss deepened and she became aware of his body over hers. She clung tightly to him, and obeyed the undeniable instinct to press her body to his. 'Oh, Lyle!' she breathed as she felt the movement of his body against her.

When he took his mouth from hers, she kept her eyes closed, while her lips parted to invite more of his kisses. Then suddenly she became aware of some strangled sound from him as the pressure of his body left hers and he wrenched himself away from her. Abruptly she opened her eyes.

Startled, she realised that Lyle was sitting on the settee, looking down at her. Looking down at her, but not with any of the tenderness and gentleness she had felt in his lips. But if she wasn't mistaken, with all the dislike and aggression that had been in him before.

Abruptly she sat up. 'What...?' she gasped in confusion.

For answer, Lyle Hetherington wiped the back of his hand insultingly across his mouth. Then he stood up and, looking arrogantly down at her, in the most insolent, cutting tone she had heard him use so far, 'If you think I'm interested in my father's leavings,' he sneered, 'then think again, sweetheart.' Kelsa's eyes were saucer-wide as, having flattened her, he turned his back on her, and strolled out.

CHAPTER THREE

EVEN while she was mentally calling Lyle Hetherington a few very unpleasant names, and hoping that somehow, somewhere he would get his come-uppance, Kelsa was still feeling shaken when she drove to work on Wednesday morning. In the hours since Lyle Hetherington had so insolently strolled out of her flat, she had re-lived again and again everything that had taken place since she had opened the door and had found him, tall and icy-eyed, standing there.

Though what stunned her so much that even the insults that had gone before seemed to dim in her mind was her reaction to him when the tenor of his kisses had changed.

Had that been *her*? Had that been her last night—that willing, passionate woman?

As she left her car, Kelsa was still trying to come to terms with how easily Lyle Hetherington had changed her, with a few expert kisses, from a woman who had very high moral values to such an eagerly participating woman. How far things might have gone had he not so abruptly called a halt she had no idea. She sincerely hoped, though, bearing in mind her strict upbringing in such matters, not to mention her own beliefs, that she would have come to her senses before much longer. She went into her office finding it something of a worry that, when she didn't even *like* the man, she couldn't be sure.

Not long afterwards, however, all such thoughts were pushed far to the background of her mind, for she had a far greater worry to contend with. For the first time, when Garwood Hetherington was always in the office before her, she discovered she had beaten him to it. Not that that particularly alarmed her, but he still hadn't arrived when shortly afterwards Nadine Anderson came in.

'No Mr Hetherington?' Nadine queried.

Kelsa shook her head. 'Do you think he's been delayed in traffic?'

'Possibly,' said Nadine, but since he was always there at least half an hour before either of them Kelsa could see that she didn't quite believe it. And she saw too that, although they'd both got on with some work, Nadine couldn't settle, when at ten o'clock she stopped what she was doing and said, 'I think I'll give Lyle a ring.' Even as she stretched out a hand to the internal phone, however, it rang, and Kelsa could tell from the conversation, from Nadine's tone as she repeated the name of a hospital, that something was very wrong.

'Was that . . . ?' she began.

'That was Mr Ford.'

'About Mr Hetherington?' Kelsa questioned urgently.

'He's in hospital—he's had a heart attack!' Nadine told her in a shocked voice.

'Oh, no!' exclaimed Kelsa. But as her concern spiralled, suddenly another thought hit her like a bolt from the blue. 'Which one?' she croaked, and when Nadine again repeated the name of the hospital, 'Not that—which Mr Hetherington?' she wanted to know with all speed.

'The man we work for—Garwood Hetherington,' said Nadine, and seemed to realise that neither of them was thinking very clearly in these initial moments of stress. Kelsa was still trying to get her thoughts together when Nadine went to repeat Ramsey Ford's information that Lyle Hetherington was at his father's bedside, and that he, Ramsey Ford, would be in touch when there was any news.

The fact that Garwood Hetherington was fighting for his life occupied more of Kelsa's thoughts than the fact that for a moment a while ago she had experienced a terrifying fear that it was Lyle Hetherington who had had a heart attack. Heart attacks were no respecters of persons, be they young or old, she knew that.

But there was no time then to do more than see that her conscience had been pricking her for having wished something fairly unpleasant to befall Lyle Hetherington. Time only to realise that that must be the reason she had felt near to fainting at the thought that it might be he who was suddenly so very ill. Time then to only fear and pray for his father, the man whom, in so short a space of knowing him, of working with him daily, she held in such high esteem and dear affection.

Neither she nor Nadine could work on anything that required too much concentration after that. But about half an hour later, while Nadine was finishing off an internal call, Kelsa reached for the phone to answer a call on an external line and was totally shattered to hear Lyle Hetherington on the other end. He waited only to hear her voice, then, 'My father's dying,' he informed her curtly. 'Get here fast!'

'M-me? I'm Kelsa...'

'He's asking for you—*move*!' Abruptly he terminated his call.

Staggered, her colour gone, her mouth open, Kelsa looked across at Nadine. 'That was Lyle Hetherington. His father's asking for me—it sounds—urgent!' she gasped—and that was when she again had evidence of Nadine's unflappability, for although Kelsa knew that she too was very fond of their employer—it would have been impossible to work so closely with him and not be, she felt—Nadine did no more than pick up the phone with the appearance of calm and ring the transport department.

'You're in no fit state to drive,' she stated, and in a matter of minutes, without questioning why it was their employer should be asking for her, Kelsa was on her way in a company car which Nadine had organised.

Kelsa tried not to think at all in that nightmare dash to the hospital. Lyle had said his father was dying, but he couldn't be—could he? It didn't seem possible! Why, only yesterday he had ruffled her hair, called her a beautiful...

Her thoughts ceased as, reaching the hospital in record time, she hurried inside. She was searching for someone to give her directions, however, when striding along a corridor towards her she saw Lyle Hetherington.

She went swiftly up to him, and he turned round—obviously he had come in search of her—not slackening his speed, so that she almost had to run to keep up with him.

A lift was waiting, and she had a chance to get her breath back as they travelled upwards. She sorely wanted to ask him for news of his father, but she knew, since the news was already grave, that she'd probably get her head bitten off if she did.

Instead, 'Your mother...?' she began, and got her head bitten off anyway.

'Is my concern!' he rapped.

'I just wondered if you'd been able to contact her,' Kelsa murmured. 'She was on a cruise, and...' The lift doors opened, and as he strode out she was left talking to the air. Somehow, though, she knew, since he was certain she was having an affair with his father, that Lyle was unlikely to allow her anywhere near his mother.

But, as she again hurried to keep up with him, she put such thoughts out of her head and, with her insides churning, she entered the private ward.

She approached the bed and saw Garwood Hetherington, his face colourless, looking not at all like the man she knew. He had various pieces of lifesaving equipment attached to him, and quietly, carefully, she took a seat in one of the two chairs placed close to the bed. Some minutes later, as if he knew she was there, he opened his eyes and looked straight at her.

'Hello,' she smiled gently.

'Hello,' he responded weakly, 'my dear—dear—girl,' then, the trace of a smile on his mouth, closed his eyes again.

Five minutes elapsed before he opened his eyes again, and then it was his son that he looked at. 'I'm so—proud—of you, Lyle,' he gasped in fractured tones, and Kelsa felt so choked that she had the hardest work to hold back the tears.

Again he closed his eyes, and a few minutes later there was a change in his breathing, and Kelsa knew, without having any previous experience of such matters, that he was falling into unconsciousness. This, all her sensitivity told her, was a time when Lyle should be alone with his father.

Quietly she rose from her chair and for a moment she stood looking down at Garwood Hetherington, then gently she touched her lips to his cheek and, having said goodbye to him she left his room.

She could not leave the hospital, though, she found, but there was a small waiting area nearby, and she went and sat in there. She lost count of time as the minutes ticked by, but with her eyes on the door of Garwood Hetherington's room, she watched the scene of activity as doctors and nurses came and went.

Her nerves were stretched taut as one nurse and then another—no longer with that hurried walk—came away from the room. When a minute later the doctor too came out, Kelsa waited only until he had disappeared down a corridor, then she left her seat.

She was standing near to the door of the room when some ten minutes later it opened again and this time Lyle Hetherington, his face stiff with strain, came out.

She looked at him as his glance flicked towards her, her eyes asking the question, and received the harsh answer, 'My father's dead.'

She had been expecting it, but it was a shock just the same. 'I'm—sorry,' she whispered huskily.

'I'll bet you are!' Lyle Hetherington grunted, and without another word he strode past her.

Kelsa felt too upset after that to go back to work. She felt choked about Garwood Hetherington dying, and hurt by Lyle's parting remark, for that must mean he thought she was sorry—but only on account of any gifts or money drying up now that his father was dead.

She was unable to face using public transport, so she took a taxi back to her flat, fully realising that her car was still in Hetheringtons' car park. She knew that once she got home she should pick up the phone and ring Nadine, but for a long while she could not do so.

Just then she felt stunned, sad and weepy at what had happened. Had she spared a thought to wonder why Mr Hetherington had asked for her—it now no longer seemed to matter why. He was dead. That lovely man was gone. He hadn't been all that old, for goodness' sake, and he'd worked so hard—it just didn't seem fair.

Later, during the early afternoon, she did attempt to put in a call to Nadine, but was told that Mrs Anderson wasn't available. It did not surprise her that Nadine was too upset to work too, and had also gone home.

By morning Kelsa was having to come to terms with her employer's passing. Though she felt he was more than just a mere employer. There had been warmth in him for those he worked with, a never-failing courtesy...

She was on a bus on her way to work, however, when, facing the fact that work without him there was not going to be the same, she suddenly, and with the force of a thunderbolt, realised that she had no need to upset herself about that. For as she recalled how Lyle Hetherington had told her icily that she wouldn't have a job for very much longer if he had anything to do with it, it occurred to her that he would be certain to be the one to succeed his father as chairman. Then she knew with equal certainty that one of his first actions on taking over would be to dismiss her! Very soon she wouldn't have a job to go to.

She got off the bus and made her way to Hetheringtons, and in the five-minute walk to her office fought a silent battle between enjoyment of the work she did, which suggested that she should try to stay on, and her pride, which insisted she should not give him the chance to say, 'On your way!' at his first opportunity.

Pride won, as she realised it had always been going to. She would, head in the air, go voluntarily—before she was pushed. Initially, though, when she and Nadine met again in the office, and in those five minutes of being without the employer they had thought so well of, they sat and discussed the sad happenings of the day before. And more minutes went by during which, perhaps because of the shock they'd both received, they were far more communicative than they had ever been before.

'It goes without saying that Lyle will be chairman now,' Nadine commented.

'I've been thinking about that,' Kelsa confessed, 'and it seems to me that, while you'll be much in demand for your expertise and knowledge of the smooth running of this office, Lyle Hetherington will probably otherwise want you to work in tandem with his PA, which means that I shall be surplus to requirements.' And while Nadine blinked at this summing up, Kelsa rushed on quickly, 'I've decided to leave.'

For quite some while then, as Nadine told her of Lyle Hetherington's reputation for hard work and how Ottilie Miller had confided at lunch in the canteen one day that she welcomed his trips abroad since it gave her a chance to catch up, they debated the issue.

'There's bound to be the same niche here for you,' Nadine assured her. 'Particularly since it's a foregone conclusion that Mr Hetherington will have left all his shares in the company to Lyle and...'

'Not to his wife?' asked Kelsa, a little surprised.

'Um...' Nadine hesitated, but then, because she had learned that Kelsa would never break a confidence, 'In point of fact, Mrs Hetherington rather resents the firm.'

'*Resents* it?'

'Resents the time Mr Hetherington gives—gave to it,' Nadine confided. 'But, apart from her having no interest in the company, she's wealthy in her own right, so she doesn't need more money, and I've an idea she positively wouldn't give a thank-you for any shares Mr Hetherington left her.'

'Oh, what a pity,' Kelsa commented, and at Nadine's querying look, 'I mean what a pity, when Mr Hetherington worked so hard, that his wife couldn't be interested in all he achieved.'

'Oh, she was interested at the start,' said Nadine, confiding, 'She lent him huge sums of money from time to time—all paid back by now, of course. But—and as you know, I've been with Mr Hetherington for seventeen years—when Lyle, against her wishes, joined the firm after university, and then started to devote as much time to it as his father, she vowed never to have another thing to do with the company, or to set foot in it again.'

'Oh, so that's why Mrs Hetherington would be more likely to feel insulted than pleased should Mr Hetherington have left her anything to do with the company,' Kelsa replied.

'Exactly,' stated Nadine, and went on, 'Though with Lyle now able to add his father's shares to his own stockholding, the board won't have a leg to stand on when next his diversification plans come up for discussion.'

'How do you mean?'

'For diversification, read expansion,' Nadine answered.

'Aren't Hetheringtons big enough already?'

'In the dog-eat-dog world of commerce one has to diversify to survive, to exploit any spare capacity,' Nadine outlined. 'So you see,' she smiled, 'you can't leave. If Lyle goes ahead with some big expansion scheme—and there's no one to stop him now that his father will have left him everything—Hetheringtons will want to take on more staff, in all areas, not lose any.'

Kelsa was almost persuaded by her argument. Against that, though, was the certain knowledge that there was one member of his staff, in the assistant to personal assistant area, whom she was certain Lyle Hetherington couldn't wait to lose.

'I'm sorry, Nadine,' she said quietly, 'but I want to go.'

Nadine studied her serious, set expression for a moment or two and perhaps read there that Kelsa was, if sad about it, determined to leave. 'I shouldn't do anything hasty,' she advised, and undermined Kelsa's determination completely by adding, 'I know Mr

Hetherington was planning a ''three-months' notice on either side'' clause in your contract,' and, when Kelsa had been thinking in terms of leaving, say, tomorrow, 'For the sake of his memory, how do you feel about staying on for three months to help me with what could be a busy change-over period?'

'Oh, Nadine!' Kelsa exclaimed, knowing she'd do anything in the memory of the super man Garwood Hetherington had been—if she were allowed.

'You can type out your resignation today if you like,' Nadine coaxed, as if to make it better, and Kelsa was sunk.

'Very well,' she agreed, and knew she was being weak when she typed out her notice and handed it over. She guessed Nadine was perhaps thinking in terms of her maybe changing her mind at some time during the next three months.

Kelsa didn't know if Lyle Hetherington had put in an appearance that day, but she thought not. But at any rate, she didn't see anything of him. Nor did she see anything of him the next day, and she went home that night having refused the invitation to dine with some young executive from Purchasing to eat a solitary dinner and to decide not to go to Drifton Edge that weekend. Whereupon she spent a weekend which was one of the bleakest she had known since her parents had died.

She awakened on Monday in a not very cheerful frame of mind and, to add to her general feeling of depression, found that her car wouldn't start. She again resorted to public transport, and rang her garage as soon as she reached her office. There followed a complex discussion in which the service manager explained how to start it and suggested she try and drive it in the next day.

'I'll see you tomorrow,' she confirmed, keeping her fingers crossed that, should she be able to start it, she would be able to nurse her car as far as the garage.

She still had the phone in her hand when the outer door opened and Mr Ford, with whom Nadine had been in frequent telephone contact since last Thursday, came in. 'Good morning,' he greeted them both, had a few words with Nadine and, with Nadine following him, walked through into what was now Mr Hetherington's old office.

Half an hour later Nadine came out alone and revealed that Lyle had requested that Ramsey Ford oversee their office for a short while. 'In the meantime,' she went on, 'Mr Ford, knowing that we'd want to anyway, has asked that you and I attend Mr Hetherington's funeral tomorrow.'

Oh, how she was tugged two ways! With her deep respect and affection for Garwood Hetherington, Kelsa did want to go. But, realising that his son would hate it if she did, she felt she shouldn't.

'I . . .' she began to refuse, but as Nadine stood there, fully expecting no opposition, Kelsa couldn't think of a single excuse for not going—not without telling Nadine all about Lyle Hetherington's suspicions. And somehow, to voice the fact that he believed she had been having an affair with his father seemed an insult to his dead father's memory. 'What time?' she asked.

Kelsa wore a grey suit to the office the next morning, having, with the help of a passing Samaritan, got her car started. She walked from the garage to her office, having been advised that there was no chance of her car being ready that evening, but she was more concerned then with the fact that she was going to Mr Hetherington's funeral that day than with her car.

Thankfully, they had an unexpected busy workload in the post that morning, which gave Kelsa little time to dwell on the matter. But when later she and Nadine left for the funeral in Nadine's car, Kelsa began to be torn in two again. It seemed essential to her that she should go and pay her last respects to her employer, but at the same time she didn't want to upset anyone, namely Lyle Hetherington, who had loved his father and who would not take kindly to seeing her there.

There was every chance that he wouldn't even notice her, she suddenly brought herself up short to decide bracingly. He would be much too preoccupied. And in any event, since Garwood Hetherington was such a well-known figure, she would most likely be lost from his sight in the mass of other people attending to pay their respects.

The funeral passed with dignity and due ceremony, and Kelsa, with sadness in her heart for Mr Hetherington's passing, saw Lyle, tall and straight, escorting a tall, aristocratic-looking woman of about sixty.

But so much for her notion that he wouldn't notice her. Because once the service was over, notice her he did. With a taut expression and with the aristocratic woman holding his arm, he walked back up the aisle of the church, and as they drew level with where she was standing—although he had been looking straight ahead—Lyle Hetherington moved his head her way a fraction and, flicking an ice-cold glance at her, looked straight through her. Kelsa knew then that she would not be called upon to work her three months' notice.

Both she and Nadine were in solemn mood as they drove back to the office. Though once there, as Nadine went over to her desk, Kelsa observed that Nadine, having worked for Garwood Hetherington for all those years, seemed about to break down.

'Why don't you go home, Nadine?' she suggested gently.

'I've a notion delayed reaction is setting in,' Nadine admitted. 'But I've got too much to do...'

'You go home,' Kelsa insisted. 'I'll see to everything here.'

'I...'

'I promise,' Kelsa smiled.

'Are you sure?'

'Certain,' Kelsa assured her.

She still had her head down at seven o'clock, but had been in touch with Security to tell them she was working late. Which was why when at ten past seven she heard the door open and someone come in she thought it was a security officer come to check if she was still there.

She looked up, a pleasant comment on her lips, only to have that comment freeze unuttered. Because the tall, still dark-suited, grey-eyed male who stood looking coldly down at her was, she knew, definitely not from Security.

Nor, as her voice died in her throat, was he waiting for her to revive it. The look in his eyes was no warmer since she had last seen him. 'Dedicated to duty, I see!' Lyle Hetherington rapped, and Kelsa guessed that if he was hurting inside then he had found just the person he was looking for to take it out on.

'Just catching up on a few things,' she said as calmly as she could, as she wondered if perhaps he had come to his father's office to say a private farewell to him.

'Your car isn't in the car park!' he snarled.

'It has a habit of playing up—it's being repaired at the moment,' she told him. She had been unaware that he knew her car, but her calm was too soon starting to fracture. And she could tell from his aggressiveness that he was hellbent on having a go at her.

As was soon proved. 'I'd have thought, with the way *you* share yourself around,' his eyes went offensively over her, 'that you'd have a car by now that wasn't "always playing up".'

At his deliberate insult, Kelsa had had it with him. She reached for her bag and abruptly stood up. She tried desperately to hang on to her temper, but knew she was not making a very good job of it. 'You can keep your sneers, *and* your gibes,' she snapped. 'I'm leaving!'

'Far be it from me to keep you,' he rapped, moving from where he was blocking her way. 'Though I doubt it will be too long before some male other than my father will,' he added as a stinging afterthought.

Kelsa almost told him not to be disgusting, but—and she was getting too angry to remember—she had an idea she had told him that before. And she swallowed hard on her fury when she also remembered the hurt that was in Lyle that day. 'Not only am I leaving this building, but, for your information, I'm leaving Hetheringtons,' she told him instead.

She didn't miss the sharp, alert look that came to his eyes, but although he had nothing insulting to come back with, mockery had entered his tones as he drawled, 'Are you, now?'

'I gave three months' notice last Thursday!' she retorted—and saw those intelligent grey eyes narrow as he reflected on that.

A moment later, though, and his aggressiveness was back in full force. 'What the hell sort of game are you playing?' he demanded angrily.

And that annoyed her. 'One which you, with your nasty suspicious mind, would quite obviously never recognise!' she flew, and would have marched out, only he moved to narrow the gap, and she had once before stood close up to him and had never forgotten it.

She took a step back, then saw that he was far more astute than she had realised. In a matter of only a couple of seconds it seemed, he had found the answer. 'For pride?' he queried. 'Pride because of...' Abruptly he broke off, and his face became dark with his own fury. 'Don't give me that,' he gritted. 'If you'd any pride you'd never have gone to bed with a man whose age...'

'Will you *stop* it!' Kelsa yelled, so infuriated by him and his vile insinuations that she couldn't take any more. And, past caring suddenly, 'For your information,' she spat hotly, 'the only person I've ever slept with is *me*!' There, she fumed, her brilliantly blue eyes flashing, chew on that!

'You're a virgin!' he scoffed, widening the gap between them again. 'And the band played believe *that* if you like!' he derided.

Kelsa had hit him once before; now she came close to hitting him again. 'I'm going home!' she threw at him angrily instead, and headed for the door.

'Want a lift?' he drawled before she could reach it, his voice loaded with mockery once more—and Kelsa turned.

'With *you*?' she scorned. 'I'd crawl rather!'

The ice was back in his voice when, his eyes taking in every furious trembling nerve of her, he snarled, 'I hope I'm there to see it!'

She turned round and went fuming on her way. By the time she had reached her flat, however, she had calmed down sufficiently to be able to realise that she still had a job to go to tomorrow—for Lyle Hetherington, astonishingly, hadn't dismissed her, had he?

CHAPTER FOUR

BY MORNING Kelsa was feeling rather ashamed that she had allowed Lyle Hetherington to goad her into getting angry. It was so unlike her to lose her temper, though. But she had to own that her reactions to him were very unlike her normal reactions to anyone else—and that had been from almost the first moment of meeting him.

She was still regretting having flared up at him as she sat in the bus going to work. Clearly yesterday—the day of his father's funeral—had been a bad day for him emotionally. And she had been so nasty. Oh, how could she?

Not that he'd been particularly pleasant to her, she rallied, as she got off the bus and went on to her office feeling decidedly out of sorts.

'Good morning, Nadine,' she greeted her, and saw that, probably on account of her shortened day yesterday, it looked as though Nadine had come in early and been at it for at least half an our.

'Good morning, Kelsa,' said Nadine, and with a smile, 'Thanks for holding the fort for me yesterday afternoon. Any problems?' she asked.

How Kelsa wished that by merely sharing her problem Nadine, with her expertise in business, could so easily solve it. 'Just a couple of queries,' she replied, and going to get some work out of her drawer, got down to business.

She was sipping a cup of coffee at around eleven when she had time to mull over the fact that, by the look of it, she still had a job. She had thought, from the way

Lyle had looked through her in the church yesterday—not to mention their row last night—that he would waste no time in giving her the order of the boot this morning.

She puzzled over that fact for some minutes, but at the end of that time could only wonder if, despite still believing what he did of her, Lyle, from love and respect for his father's memory, had decided to allow her to work her notice out. Had he reached that decision by thinking that since maybe his father had cared for her, he should honour that, when three months would pass soon enough anyway?

Kelsa was still wondering about it when the phone rang, and she donned her professional manner to answer it. 'Brian Rawlings here, of Burton and Bowett,' the man who was calling introduced himself, and while Kelsa at once tabbed them 'Company solicitors' and prepared to pass him courteously over to Nadine, 'Am I speaking to Miss Stevens?' he enquired, courteous and professional himself.

'Yes,' she answered, stretching out a hand ready to transfer the call to Nadine's phone.

Suddenly, though, her hand stilled, because, every inch a lawyer as he made certain that he was speaking to the party he wanted to speak to, he enquired, 'Miss Kelsa Primrose March Stevens?'

'Yes,' she replied, mystified and even a little amused.

Her amusement fell abruptly away, however, as he stated, 'It's important that you present yourself at our offices at two o'clock today.' And while Kelsa was blinking at that, 'Do you know where they are?' he asked pleasantly.

'Yes, but—but...' Her brain cleared to allow her to form a sentence. 'I'm sorry to be so vague,' she rallied, 'but can you tell me what for? I mean, what's it in connection with?' So far as she could remember, Nadine and Mr Hetherington were the only ones who always dealt with anything to do with Burton and Bowett.

'The will,' he explained. 'Mr Garwood Hetherington's will.'

'His *will*!' she exclaimed, noticing that Nadine had looked up to see if she needed any help.

Kelsa shook her head, and tuned in to hear Brian Rawlings answer, 'I apologise for not writing to you, I intended to do that today, but this morning is my first morning back from holidaying abroad, and it was only then that I learned of Mr Hetherington's passing.'

'You—were going to write to me?' Kelsa picked out of what he had said, wondering why he still couldn't write to her and what was so important that she go and see him at two.

'Indeed I was, and will, of course,' he stated obscurely. 'But I had a telephone call from Mrs Edwina Hetherington this morning, and she's insisting that the contents of her deceased husband's will are disclosed today.'

'I—understand,' Kelsa said slowly, but she didn't, not at all, not a bit of it.

'Good! So you'll be here at two, Miss Stevens?'

'Er—yes,' she agreed.

'I'll look forward to seeing you then,' he murmured politely, and Kelsa put her phone down, to stare at Nadine in some consternation.

'Everything all right?' asked Nadine, looking ready to help, whatever the problem was.

'That was Mr Rawlings of Burton and Bowett.'

'Oh, he's back from holiday,' Nadine commented.

'Back, and wants me to go and see him at two,' Kelsa told her.

She admired Nadine more than ever for her unflappability, when she too must be thinking it was in connection with company business. 'He wants to see *you* at two?' she questioned mildly—and Kelsa gave her a brief outline of how the conversation had gone. Whereupon Nadine remarked that it sounded as though Mr Hetherington had left Kelsa a bequest in his will.

'Have you had a telephone call too from Mr Rawlings?' was Kelsa's natural question after that.

'No,' said Nadine, and, when she could see that Kelsa was starting to look worried, 'But don't let that upset you. I've been aware since you came to work with me that while Mr Hetherington held my office skills in high esteem, he seemed to have a special empathy with you. Now don't worry,' she went on quickly, 'he's probably left you some small token out of that empathy the two of you shared. Just present yourself at Burton and Bowett at two, and then...' she smiled '...hare back here and tell me all about it.'

Kelsa was glad of Nadine's calmness in the hours leading up to lunchtime, because several thoughts had occurred to her during that time—one of them being that, since she hadn't known Mr Hetherington all that long, the will in which her name featured could have only recently been drawn up. And while at one point Kelsa had been certain that she would rather Mr Hetherington hadn't singled her out to leave her anything, she now, recalling him with affection, realised that she would quite like some small memento of him.

Against that, though, it seemed that in order to claim that small token she would have to be there at the will-reading today. There too, if she had worked it out correctly, would be Mrs Edwina Hetherington, Garwood Hetherington's aristocratic-looking wife. But while Kelsa reckoned that meeting Mrs Hetherington presented no problem, she wished, since Lyle Hetherington was bound to be there too, that she could say the same about him!

For she was certain, knew it for a fact, that Lyle Hetherington would be furious that through his father's will his mother should have to spend so much as a minute in the same room as the woman he thought was his father's mistress.

By the time one o'clock arrived Kelsa had formed the view that they could carry on the will-reading without her. Brian Rawlings had said he would write to her anyway, so let him do that.

Having made her mind up on that score, she went and had a bite to eat in the canteen, and afterwards walked down to the garage in anticipation of collecting her car. It was as she was waiting to see the assistant service manager, however—the service manager being at lunch—that suddenly the moral fibre of her upbringing got to her, and she started to wonder, grief, when had she become such a coward?

It wasn't as if Mrs Hetherington thought she was her husband's mistress, was it, for goodness' sake? It was only Lyle who thought it, and she had told him repeatedly that there was not a thing going on between her and his father. If Lyle Hetherington had an evil mind, then that was his problem, not hers.

Having started to get quite cross at the label which Lyle had so unwarrantedly stuck on her, Kelsa determined she wouldn't lie down under it. She wouldn't be a coward, she wouldn't let him make a coward of her!

'I've come for my car!' she told the assistant service manager quite belligerently when he finally got round to her.

'I'm—er—afraid it isn't quite ready yet,' he told her timidly, and Kelsa immediately wanted to apologise for her belligerent tone.

'It's the red Fiesta,' she told him hopefully in a more gentle fashion.

'I know, Miss Stevens,' he said more confidently, 'but it still isn't ready.'

That, Kelsa thought as she walked away from the garage, was that. Without her car there was no way she was going to make it to Messrs Burton and Bowett for two o'clock. She looked at her watch and realised she'd be hard pushed to make it to Burton and Bowett's for two o'clock *with* her car.

She started to walk back to Hetheringtons, resigned to the fact that, while everything inside her suddenly revolted against being stuck with the label of 'coward', she would be ignoring Brian Rawlings' phone call of that morning.

She had almost reached Hetheringtons, though, and had taken a short cut down a side street, when there, in an area where taxis were seldom seen, she espied a taxi coming towards her. It was meant!

In a flash she had flagged it down. In seconds she had given the driver her required destination—and was starting to feel all churned up inside again.

When the taxi dropped her off at five past two outside the solicitors' offices, Kelsa knew she need not really go inside. But go inside she did. And it seemed then, as she went up to the reception desk and told them her name and whom she was there to see, that since Garwood Hetherington had been kind enough to remember her in his will she should make whatever effort was required to claim it.

'Oh, yes, Miss Stevens,' said the young woman behind the desk. 'Mr Rawlings has asked you go up immediately you arrive. They're all there, just waiting for you.'

Oh, grief, Kelsa thought as, following the receptionist's directions, she climbed a couple of flights of stairs and made for Mr Rawlings' room. For while she had hoped to slip discreetly in and merge with all the other legatees there, it seemed that Mr Rawlings was waiting until the last one, however lowly, had arrived before he began the proceedings.

There was still time for her to turn tail, but she wouldn't, not now, she knew that. And, finding the door she was looking for, she went forward and knocked firmly on its panels.

It was opened at once by a man of average build, in his mid-thirties, with a charming manner. 'Miss Stevens?' he queried.

'That's right.'

'Brian Rawlings,' he introduced himself, holding out his hand. 'Come along in.' He smiled as they shook hands, and led the way into his office where, to Kelsa's great surprise, there were only three other people—Lyle Hetherington, the woman whom he had escorted yesterday, and who she was sure was his mother, and another woman, aged somewhere in her forties.

Kelsa was not the only one who was surprised, she realised in those first initial moments, for while all she felt from Lyle was ice-cold hostility, his mother looked exceedingly put out, while the other woman looked at her with great interest.

'Who is this woman?' Mrs Hetherington demanded imperiously, before Brian Rawlings could offer to tell her, and Kelsa knew at once that she wouldn't like to get on the wrong side of her. 'And why is she here?'

'This is Miss Stevens. Miss Kelsa Stevens,' he introduced her, while Kelsa suddenly decided she shouldn't have come, and concentrated her attention on a yachting picture on the wall for a moment or two while, firmly, Brian Rawlings continued, 'And Miss Stevens is here for the same reason as everyone else—for the reading of the will.'

'You mean she *features* in it?' Mrs Hetherington exclaimed.

'All will become plain shortly, Mrs Hetherington,' he answered, and attempted to introduce Kelsa around. 'Miss Stevens, this is Mrs Garwood Hetherington,' he began. Mrs Hetherington didn't deign to offer her hand, but Kelsa hadn't thought she would. 'Mrs Ecclestone——' he turned to the other woman '—Miss Stevens.' In Kelsa's view Mrs Ecclestone seemed to be a little shaken, though whether at Mrs Hetherington's attitude or the fact that she too didn't like her being there, Kelsa couldn't decide. But when it seemed that Mrs Ecclestone might extend her hand, Brian Rawlings was looking from Kelsa to Lyle and observing, 'I don't think there's any need to introduce Miss Stevens, is there, Lyle? Miss Stevens works...'

'None whatever!' he clipped, his glance on her withering, then ignoring her completely. 'When you're ready, Brian,' he hinted.

At that none too subtle reminder of why they were there, Brian Rawlings invited Kelsa to take the only other vacant chair in the room, other than his own round the other side of the desk, and when they were both seated he began the proceedings.

'This is the last will and testament of Garwood David Hetherington, dated...' he paused, ahemmed a little, and revealed that the will had been made only recently.

'He made a new will?' exclaimed Mrs Hetherington, her cultured tones sounding as if she wasn't very pleased about that. Clearly she knew nothing about it and had not been consulted by her husband. And, referring to the date Brian Rawlings had mentioned, 'But that was only two weeks ago yesterday,' she worked out.

'Er—quite so,' Brian Rawlings agreed pleasantly, but, though smiling courteously, he seemed to think they might be there all day if he didn't hurry things along. 'I'll deal with the minor bequests first.' Good, Kelsa thought—as soon as she heard why she had been asked to come here she could go.

Only it wasn't quite as simple as that. For, since the amounts and effects were being announced on a rising scale, she began to feel rather uncomfortable when amounts of one thousand pounds and then two thousand pounds were dealt with, and her name had not been mentioned. When, preceding her, Nadine Anderson's name and an even larger amount than two thousand pounds was quoted—for Nadine's loyal and devoted service all these years—Kelsa started to grow extremely apprehensive. With the bequests being referred to in order of ascending value—what on earth had Mr Hetherington left her?

Starting to feel a little pink around the ears as Brian Rawlings went on, Kelsa could only hope that her name had been included in the will as an afterthought. Maybe tacked on at the end was a note to the effect that Mr Hetherington wanted her to have some trinket, an ornament or some such.

'That concludes the minor bequests.' Brian Rawlings looked up from the parchment in his hands. Kelsa's mouth formed an 'O', but, just as she was about to state that there must be some mistake and that she shouldn't be there, and would they excuse her, the solicitor, as if wanting to get this over quickly, was going on, 'To my sister Alicia Helen Ecclestone, of...' Kelsa blanked off for a moment in the panic of wondering what was going on. Surely... '...my wife, Edwina Sibilla Hetherington...' Kelsa heard Brian Rawlings' voice going on, while every nerve in her body started to reject and deny the notion that her own name might be the next one he uttered.

The bequest to Mrs Hetherington, with some mention that she had her own fortune, was detailed and lengthy. She was to have the house, and parkland which no doubt in due time, along with her personal estate, would go to their son. There were other various effects and properties she was to have. And then Brian Rawlings was clearing his throat.

Then, 'To my beloved son Carlyle Garwood Hetherington,' he began, going on to give Lyle Hetherington's address in Berkshire, but to Kelsa's astonishment, he went on, 'and to my dear Kelsa Primrose March Stevens of...' despite the gasp which Kelsa felt came from the other two women, as well as herself, at the mention of her name in the same sentence as Lyle's, he went on determinedly and, after giving her address, read, 'I leave jointly, and in equal portions, all my business interests, all my stocks and shares in the Hetherington Group, all my——' That was as far as he got before pandemonium broke out.

'*No*!' Lyle was on his feet in an instant, and forcefully and furiously, he was the first to erupt. 'This is preposterous! Quite outrageous!'

'Utterly scandalous!' Mrs Hetherington was on her feet too. 'It can't be legal! We'll contest it!' she declared venomously.

'It is legal,' Brian Rawlings tried to pacify them quietly. 'And I'm afraid that to contest your late husband's will would do no good, Mrs Hetherington. I was away on holiday when Mr Hetherington came to see a senior partner to sign his new will. Mr Wendell, and the witnesses, have not the smallest doubt that he was of sound mind and under no duress. In fact, Mr Wendell assures me that he had never seen him looking more content. So...'

'So nothing!' snapped Mrs Hetherington. 'My son has worked every bit as hard as his father for that place. It's iniquitous that *that* woman should...'

That woman! Kelsa had been sitting feeling too deeply shocked to utter so much as a squeak. But those two slighting words, aimed at her, got through, and, feeling the hostility towards her, she got to her feet too, and made for the door.

Pandemonium was still going on when, feeling completely stunned and totally disbelieving of any of it, she left the room and closed the door after her.

Had she been capable of thinking at all as she reeled down the first flight of stairs, she would have said that there was too much going on for anyone to have noticed her slipping out from the room. But, as she reached a small landing and prepared to go down the next flight of stairs, a fierce angry hand on her arm swung her round, and she looked up, startled, into a pair of burning grey eyes. That was when she realised that Lyle Hetherington had not missed her departure.

Not only had he noticed her leaving the room, though, but, looking furious enough to throttle her, he had come after her and, his grip on her threatening to cut off her circulation, '*Now* tell me there was nothing going on between you and him!' he thundered with barely contained rage.

The intensity of his fury was quite alarming, but Kelsa, with what powers of judgement she could find, realised that now was not the time to repeat, *yet again*, that she had never been his father's mistress. Not certain that he might not throttle her yet if she so much as said one peep in her defence, Kelsa wrenched violently out of his hold and, finding she was free, lost no time in racing down the next flight of stairs. To her relief, he did not pursue her.

Once she was out on the pavement she was undecided where to make for. Instinctively she wanted to be alone. Against that, though, they were busy in the office, and she had already had some time off.

For Nadine's sake, Kelsa grabbed a taxi and returned to the Hetherington building. In a daze she reached her office, then realised, when Nadine said, 'Hello—heavens, you look dreadful!' and, after a pause, 'Want to tell me about it?' that she sorely needed someone to confide in.

'You're not going to believe this—I'm having trouble taking it in myself, but...'

Not many minutes later and Nadine was looking in a state of shock herself. 'I can't believe it!' she gasped.

'How do you think *I* feel?' Kelsa answered.

'How did Lyle take it?' Nadine asked what Kelsa realised was a perfectly natural question.

'As though he could cheerfully have throttled me!'

'Oh, dear,' murmured Nadine, and, having heard that Mrs Hetherington might be ready to aid and abet her son if he was thinking of murder, 'What was Brian Rawlings doing while all this was going on?'

'Trying to calm things down, I think. Everything was such a bombshell to me that I wasn't taking much in—more acting on auto-pilot,' Kelsa explained. 'Though since he and Lyle Hetherington are on first-name terms, not to mention the vast amount of business we put their way, he can't hope to be as impartial as he was trying to be.'

'He and Lyle have been pals since schooldays,' Nadine supplied—then broke off when the phone on her desk rang. 'Hello, Mr Ford, how are you?' she heard her say, and as she devoted her professionalism to taking down some notes from Ramsey Ford, and to giving him some answers he wanted, Kelsa pulled some work forward and stared down at it.

But it was hopeless. A lot of Nadine's professionalism had brushed off on to her in the short time she had been working with her. But as words and figures danced meaninglessly in front of her eyes, she had to face the fact that she was still in shock.

'It's no good,' she told Nadine when she came off the phone, 'my brain seems to have died on me.'

'I'm not surprised!' Nadine smiled sympathetically.

'Do you mind if I go home?'

'Will you be all right? You're still very pale.'

'I'll be fine,' Kelsa assured her, and left the Hetherington building to realise just how disorientated she was when, in the car park, she was unable to see her car and was striving to remember where she had parked it when she recalled that it was still in the garage.

It seemed a good idea then to concentrate on one thing at a time and, first things being first, she decided to walk down to the garage to pick up her vehicle—if it was ready. The entrance to the car park was nearer to the way she wanted to go, however, and she had just crossed to that part when in sped a long sleek black Jaguar, very nearly knocking her down.

Instinctively she jumped out of its path, but, as it stopped and she took a few paces which brought her up to the driver's window, the window was slid open and, her fears confirmed, Kelsa found herself looking into the hostile eyes of Lyle Hetherington.

Like her, he had had something of a shock that day. But one look at his enraged expression was all she needed to see to know that it wouldn't have bothered him one tiny bit had he indeed run over her. Suddenly, though, some of her deserted spirit came roaring back to life.

'I'll leave sooner than three months if you feel that bad about it!' she exploded, down but not ready to be carried out of the ring yet.

But she still wasn't ready for it as he snarled, 'Why leave?' his malevolent look volcanic. 'You *own* half the bloody place!'

She was reeling yet again, but even as she gasped at that remark she was battling to find some acid retort. Though the best she could do was to stick her nose in the air and retort haughtily, 'I hadn't thought of that!'

'Like hell you hadn't!' he blasted her eardrums, and seemed so incensed then that whether she was standing close to his car or whether she wasn't he paid no heed, but, as if needing action, put his foot on the accelerator and sped past her.

Swine! she thought, and was shaking so badly from the encounter that she afterwards had no recollection of walking to the garage.

CHAPTER FIVE

GOSSIP at the office about Kelsa's inheritance was rife over the next couple of days. 'I believe congratulations are in order,' Ramsey Ford, who was about the same age as Garwood Hetherington, had stopped by her desk on Friday to comment courteously.

'Thank you,' she murmured, looking at his wise, clever face. So far as she could tell, he looked sincere.

'I don't suppose you intend to stay on as Nadine's assistant?' he further commented, his smile as courteous as his manner.

If he was hinting, though, that with her new wealth and stockholding in the company she should be looking for a seat on the board, Kelsa didn't rise to it, but merely answered pleasantly, 'I haven't any plans at the moment other than to work with Nadine for a few months while things settle down.'

'Good.' He gave her another smile, and went on his way.

It was that same Friday that, although they were very busy, only one subject seemed to dominate any conversation she and Nadine managed to have. 'Still in shock?' asked Nadine as they took five minutes out for an afternoon cup of tea.

'It's so much to take in,' Kelsa sighed. 'It still seems incredible.' And, talking yet more shock out of her system, 'I was fond of Mr Hetherington, of course.'

'One couldn't work daily with him and not grow attached to him,' Nadine agreed understandingly.

'But, up until about six weeks ago I'd never met him. It was only because he remembered my name that he included me in the group you interviewed when...' Something in Nadine's expression caused Kelsa to break off. 'Have I said something wrong?' she queried.

'Er—perhaps I shouldn't be telling you this,' Nadine answered thoughtfully, 'but, in point of fact, you were the *only* one I interviewed.'

'I...' Kelsa couldn't make head or tail of that statement. Be it only an assistant to an assistant, it was a highly prized and most confidential job. 'I don't understand,' she had to confess.

'No more did I. But Mr Hetherington never did anything without a reason, so when he told me your name and said I should interview you but that—er—whether you shaped up or not I was to give you the job, I...'

'What?' Kelsa exclaimed, shaken again, and beginning to wonder if there was any end to the shocks she had received since her employer had died.

'Don't worry,' Nadine assured her quickly, 'you've more than proved your worth since you've worked with me.'

But Kelsa was worried, though all she could come back with was, 'You do *know* that there was nothing—er—going on between me and Mr Hetherington. That I wasn't having an affair with him?'

'Knowing him, knowing you, I'm certain you weren't,' Nadine assured her.

'I wish Lyle Hetherington were as easy to convince,' Kelsa sighed.

'He thinks... Oh, dear,' Nadine broke off. But after a moment she added, 'Well, you can hardly expect...' She hesitated, to go on a moment later, 'To be fair, Kelsa, he has had a gigantic shock.' And while Kelsa forbore to tell her that Lyle had accused her of having an affair with his father *before* his father had died and the contents of his will were made known, Nadine was continuing, 'Your inheriting the way you have is bound to seriously disrupt his future plans.'

'How?' Kelsa gasped.

'How? Easy. While he'll have had his own shares before his father left him half of his holding, that still won't give him the overall control of the company that he needs.'

'Would he have had a fifty-one-per-cent holding had his father left him everything?' Kelsa questioned, not knowing too much about the higher working of such matters, but having grasped that he would need that much.

'Probably more,' Nadine guessed. 'While I don't know the ifs, ands or buts of Lyle's diversification plans, I'd say he'll probably need a whole lot of money to put them into effect. Now he's lost the strength of his father's vote you, Kelsa, have, I believe, the power to block him.'

'Good heavens!' Kelsa exclaimed, and went home that night with a whole lot of thinking to do that weekend.

She again did not go down to Drifton Edge, and by Monday morning she was more than ready to admit that, while she had learned a lot since working on the top floor, she was a babe in arms when it came to the intricacies of big business. Saturday's post had brought a fat envelope from Messrs Burton and Bowett, solicitors. Inside there had been a letter from Brian Rawlings setting out along with all the whys and wherefores a staggering list of her assets, finance and shares, with an assurance that any small problem or query, and she must not hesitate to contact him.

Query? It would take a year for her to dissect everything!

She put the envelope and its contents away after an hour of sorting through it, then went for a walk to try to clear her head.

It was while she was out walking, however, and again thinking how she would need a twelvemonth to understand everything about her new finances, that she realised it would probably take Messrs Burton and Bowett a year or more to sort everything at their end. What with the death duties and capital gains tax she'd heard about, she started to form the opinion that Burton and Bowett were going to have their work cut out.

For the first time in an age she could feel herself start to relax. And it was then that she was able to reach the conclusion that since a whole year was likely to elapse before anything happened, she would take her time in making a decision about what best to do.

It had taken some while for the enormous shock she had received to wear off. On starting to recover, though, her first reaction had been to want to tell the solicitors that she didn't want the money, or the shares, or anything else. But then, on Friday, Nadine had said, 'But Mr Hetherington never did anything without reason', and those words had been spinning round and round in her head ever since.

She guessed that the shock she had received had been such that she hadn't asked herself that why, why, why? question before. Because it now plagued her, wouldn't let her go, and she knew she wouldn't rest until she did know why. Though, try as she might, she could come up with no answer other than that they had got on well together, had seemed to share a special empathy—and that Mr Hetherington possibly felt the same affection for her that she felt for him.

Which, she owned as she drove to the office, was just not anywhere near a good enough reason why he should have left her half his vast wealth. Nor why...

Kelsa was still puzzling at it as she got some work out and Nadine came in. 'You didn't tell me Mr Hetherington had remembered *me* in his will,' she mentioned pleasantly once they had exchanged greetings.

'Sorry,' Kelsa apologised, 'I wasn't taking it all in. Did you have a letter too on Saturday?'

Nadine nodded. 'Notifying me of Mr Hetherington's bequest. I haven't had it yet—the money, I mean,' she smiled, 'nor do I expect to for ages,' she added, which was much in line with Kelsa's own thinking. 'But it's a nice feeling to know that he thought of me.'

They settled down to work, but half an hour later the door opened and Lyle Hetherington strode in, his grim expression warning Kelsa that he too had received official notification on Saturday of how his father's estate had been left.

Kelsa's heartbeat immediately quickened when, with a nod of greeting to Nadine, he turned to her and stated flatly, 'I need to talk to you!'

Nadine tactfully got up and left the two of them alone, which threw Kelsa for a moment. But though she felt somehow disturbed by him, and awkward about the way his father had left things, that still didn't make her anybody's doormat.

'Fire away,' she therefore invited coolly, and saw immediately that he wasn't too thrilled with her or her tone.

'Not *here*!' he gritted impatiently. 'We can't talk here. I'll meet you for dinner tonight. Seven-th——'

'As it happens, I *am* free this evening,' she cut in, holding down an amazed feeling at the fluttery sensation that took her—just as though she was attracted to him and would like to have dinner with him, for goodness' sake! 'Whatever it is you want to talk to me about,' she went on, knowing quite well what it was, but deciding she felt quite cross that, after the diabolical way he'd treated her, he thought she would break bread with him, 'I prefer not to have my digestion spoiled.' It amazed her that he still stood there without throttling her—though from the way his hands clenched by his sides as if he was fighting for control, she guessed he came close. 'If you want to call at my flat for five minutes when you're free here, that's OK by me,' she offered.

Her answer was the slamming of the door behind him. Temper, temper! she thought, then realised she was shaking like a leaf from the encounter. Oh, devil take her tongue, why had she invited him to her flat?

She had calmed down some minutes later, however. Sufficient in any event to realise that since he didn't want to discuss anything with her at the office, and since she wouldn't dine with him, short of having a 'chat' in the street, she had rather limited the options.

Her flat, she realised, was where it would have to be. Since she doubted he would be any more pleasant to her than he had been, though, she didn't want to thank him for suggesting they talk over a meal—as if considering that some restaurant or hotel dining-room would be fair neutral ground.

Oh, to the devil with him! she fumed crossly, something about him eating away at her. She was never more pleased to see Nadine when the door opened and she came in.

'All clear?' she asked.

'He wants to talk—but not here,' Kelsa revealed. 'I suggested my place.'

'Well, we don't need two guesses to know the subject under discussion,' said Nadine, and concentrated her energies on the work she had been doing before she had been interrupted.

Shortly after that Mr Ford came and did a stint in the other office. But he wasn't Mr Hetherington, and when Nadine came out after having been closeted in there with him for some fifteen minutes or so and through the open doorway Kelsa saw him sitting behind Mr Hetherington's desk, she felt quite choked.

All in all, she was glad to be busy. For one thing, it gave her little time to dwell on Lyle Hetherington's intended call that evening. Not that he had verbally accepted her offhand invitation that he could come for five minutes, but Kelsa knew he'd be there. As Mrs Hetherington had said, he'd worked hard for the business—it meant a lot to him.

Kelsa broke from her usual routine when she arrived home that evening. First she showered, then she applied the small amount of make-up she used, and, even while she was berating herself for being so moronic—grief, as if he'd notice; as if she cared!—she brushed her long blonde hair into its usual style and rejected her usual jeans in favour of a smart pair of trousers and a silk blouse.

Her insides were so churned up, she couldn't entertain making herself anything to eat, so she gave herself up to wondering at what time he might arrive. The one and only other time Lyle had been to her flat it had been around eight-thirty, she recalled. Against that, though, she had an idea that he had been going to suggest dinner at seven-thirty—so what time *would* he call?

Kelsa was ready at seven and was wishing for the thousandth time that she had suggested a specific time rather than her 'when you're free'. Had she been anything like as calm underneath as she had tried to appear on the surface, she realised she might well have suggested a certain time.

Her thoughts blanked off for a while as her mind sped back to the other time Lyle had called at her flat—and how he had made her senseless with his kisses. Where had her strict upbringing been then? She gulped at the memory—she had never so much as dreamed she could respond to any man in such a way, that she could want any man in the way she had wanted Lyle then.

She was sitting with a cup of coffee when all at once it occurred to her that maybe it was that strict moral upbringing that decreed it was not right to just forgo everything Mr Hetherington had willed to her without first finding out why he'd done it.

Once again Kelsa was on the merry-go-round of trying to fathom out why, with no more success than before, when her doorbell sounded, and even though she had been expecting it, she nearly jumped out of her skin.

Striving for composure, she walked to the door, but she needed to have another second in which to take a deep and steadying breath before she reached for the door catch and turned it.

She supposed it was natural in the circumstances that her heart should race a little as she saw the tall, business-suited male standing there. Since, however, she was certain he was ready to dispense with any greeting, she did not offer him one. 'Come in,' she invited. But, striving to at least start out politely, anyway, she enquired, 'May I offer you coffee?'

His initial answer was to stare coldly into her beautiful blue eyes. But after several moments of silently looking down at her, he replied curtly, 'The sooner I say what I've come to say, the sooner I can get to my home.'

From that—while not missing the hardly veiled hint that he couldn't bear to be in her company in her home—

she guessed she would be talked at rather than talked with. 'If it's going to be brief, we'll both stand,' she found enough spirit to hint.

'After you,' he grunted, and waited while she took a seat in her one easy chair, then lowered his length to sit on her settee. 'I take it you have now been notified in writing of the contents of my father's will,' he began without preamble.

'I had a letter setting everything out on Saturday,' she agreed. 'Well, everything that concerns me,' she added—then confessed, without knowing why she should confide in him, 'It all seems extremely involved, and I can't say I can begin to understand a...' Her voice trailed off when she could see from the look on his face that he had no doubts whatsoever that, should she find anything to do with her new-found wealth in any way complicated, in his view she would have sprinted off to the solicitors first thing that morning. Since she'd been at her desk when he'd come at nine-thirty to see her, she guessed that was all the endorsement he needed that she had everything nicely, avariciously understood, thank you very much. 'So,' she snapped, tilting her chin aggressively, suddenly not feeling very kindly disposed to this cynical monster, 'I can handle my problems. What's yours?'

The narrowing of his eyes at her tone, her insolent manner, showed that she wasn't his favourite person either, just then. Well, tough—she was getting just a little tired of his attitude anyway.

'You're not dim, Miss Stevens,' he rapped. 'My problem is obvious.' She saw him glance at the long slender column of her throat, and wondered if she had been all that clever in shutting herself in with him—might he yet throttle her? There was no doubt that to do so would give him enormous satisfaction. 'But,' he clipped,

'I can get to grips with it, if...' a muscle jerked in his temple, and somehow she just *knew* that what he was about to say was sticking in his throat. But, manfully, having come to see her at all, he swallowed what was sticking in his throat, and concluded tersely, '...if you will hang fire.'

She had no idea what he was talking about but, if he was asking a favour—and she rather thought he was—then did he have a lot to learn about asking favours! 'Hang fire?' she queried. 'I—er—can you be more specific?' she enquired, and received one of his withering looks for her sins—he was rather good at those.

But since she still did not have a clue what he meant, she just sat there quietly, her eyes on his unfriendly though undeniably good-looking face. He gave her a straight, tough look, then began to lay it on the line, clearly holding back sarcasm only with the utmost difficulty.

'You won't have been working with my father and Nadine Anderson without having some idea that I'm working towards quite a large expansion plan within the next couple of years.'

'I've heard something of the sort,' she agreed quietly.

'So you'll know without my having to tell you, I'd have thought,' he inserted, sarcasm rearing, 'that I need all the backing I can get for that venture.'

Was he asking her to vote her shares on his side? Did she even have a vote? She had no idea. 'So?' she murmured, having tried once to tell him her difficulty in comprehending everything, and not prepared to invite another of his lofty looks.

'So,' he rapped, not liking her any better, she could tell, 'since for the company's future well-being it's vital that I secure all the finance I can raise—it will leave me hard pressed for extra finance.'

'You—need *extra* finance?' she asked, and got her ears singed for her trouble.

'Don't play dumb, Miss Stevens!' he erupted sharply. 'It's tough enough to have to come here to ask you to hang back before you start to milk the company until I'm in a financial position to buy your...'

'Milk the company?' she interrupted, her expression so genuinely startled that for the first time Lyle Hetherington seemed to give a little credence to her.

'Sell off any of the assets my father left you,' he explained, his look no longer totally hostile, nor angry, but considering. 'Should you dispose of any of your shares before...'

'I didn't know I could!' Kelsa exclaimed in surprise.

His look stilled. 'You haven't tried?' he questioned, and while there was that toughness about him that said he was more than ready for her if she was leading him up the garden path, Kelsa could see that he was neither mocking nor sarcastic. And suddenly she began to take heart and feel a lot better.

'Heavens, no!' she told him openly. 'I never anticipated any of the paperwork involved in Mr Hetherington's estate being settled in under twelve months anyway. And,' she thought she'd better tell him while he seemed in the least prepared to believe anything she might say, 'I wouldn't dream of touching a penny of what Mr Hetherington left me, anyhow. Not——'

'Oh, come on!' he jibed furiously. His belief in anything she might say was obviously very short-lived. 'That——'

Suddenly they were both on their feet, Kelsa as angry as he as she cut in, 'Will you *shut up* and let me finish!'

'The floor's yours—I'm on my way!' he slammed back, and was already on his way to the door when, frustrated beyond enduring, Kelsa went after him.

'*Will you listen to me*!' she yelled, her eyes flashing fury as, her temper truly lost, she caught hold of his arm.

Lyle Hetherington halted, then turned, a fierce furious look in his eyes, as he stared down into the sparking blue fury of hers. His glance then went to the hold she still had on his arm. Abruptly she took her hand away from him. Then, staring at her pink-cheeked and angry face, 'So I'm listening,' he clipped.

'So listen—hear me out!' she lost no time in getting started. 'I'm good at my job because I'm familiar with it. And in the short time I've worked with Nadine Anderson I've learned a tremendous amount. But I'm not familiar with your job, so I've no understanding of it. And that applies to Brian Rawlings' job, and any other job I haven't been trained for. So even though, as you've said, I'm not dim, since I've had nothing to do with stocks and shares, nor assets such as your father left me, I have little understanding of them either.' She paused for breath.

'Is that *it*?' Lyle gritted, clearly unimpressed.

'I haven't finished *yet*!' Kelsa came back, glaring at him for his impatience. 'When I said I wouldn't dream of touching a penny of the money, the assets if you like, that Mr Hetherington bequeathed to me, I meant it, because,' she went on firmly although it looked as though she might again get her head bitten off for her trouble, 'because *I* don't understand, either, why he left anything to me!'

'You surely don't want me to draw you a picture!' Lyle, his tone stinging, hurled at her before she could take another breath.

'*Hear me out*!' she shrieked, coming close, regardless of the consequences last time, to punching his head. He shrugged, and Kelsa set off again while he was still there.

'Not until I know *why*, will I touch anything of what he left me! Because what I can't understand is why Mr Hetherington left me anything at all.'

He didn't believe her, she could see it; it was all there in the stiff, doubting stance of him. 'Is that it now—have you finished?'

'Yes, I've finished,' she answered, her anger suddenly gone.

'You still insist on calling my father "Mr Hetherington"?'

'It's what I called him at the office.'

'And out of it.'

Kelsa took a deep and steadying breath. It was either that or hit the doubting swine. 'There were very few times when I was out of the office with your father but on those few occasions he was still Mr Hetherington to me.'

'You're still trying to maintain that there was nothing between you but business?' he questioned toughly.

'No, I'm not saying that,' she said, and took a step back at the sudden look of rage that came over him at what she seemed to be confessing. 'And before you get mad and accusatory,' she spurted out hurriedly, 'your father was a marvellous man to work for, always kind and courteous, so much so that I'd defy anybody not to grow fond of him.'

'So—you were fond of him,' he said tautly.

She nodded. 'We got on well. Perhaps he was the same with everyone—I don't know, but...' she felt foolish having to trot it out, especially to his disbelieving son, but, having been brought up to 'tell the truth and shame the devil', she refused to deny that, 'I felt we had a special sort of empathy sometimes.'

'How sweet!' he interjected acidly, and Kelsa's right hand itched.

'It *was* sweet!' she exploded. 'I got on extremely well with your father.'

'I'll say!'

'He liked me!' She ignored the barb and went racing on before he could sling in another of his vitriolic comments. 'And he liked me—must have done, to have left me so much. But——' suddenly her anger faded again '—there was never anything more than that. I swear it,' she stated sincerely.

'You're saying that my father never visited this flat?' he questioned, when he knew full well that he had.

'Only the one time when he gave me a lift home, and then remembered——'

'That he had a phone call to make,' Lyle cut in icily.

'He *did*!' she protested. 'My car has a habit of breaking down, and that night...'

'Nor have you ever dined with him, I'm sure,' he sliced harshly through what she was saying.

'You're obviously referring to that night a couple of weeks ago. That night you saw us...' Lyle had been there with a gorgeous brunette hanging on to his arm, Kelsa remembered and, most oddly, she felt an emotion shoot through her that, had she not known better, she would have thought was a dart of jealousy. Nonsense! she scoffed, and went on hurriedly, 'We'd worked late that night. The three of us...'

'Three of you?'

'Nadine Anderson was there too,' Kelsa explained. 'Nadine has recently become engaged to be married—well, I suppose she's not yet used to having a ring on her finger again or something. Anyhow, she'd gone back to the powder-room to collect the ring she'd forgotten to put back on again when she'd washed her hands...' Suddenly Kelsa came to an abrupt stop. 'Oh, what's the use!' she sighed dispiritedly, and turning her back on

Lyle Hetherington, she walked back to the centre of her sitting-room. She'd had it with him. She'd tried to explain, but he would have none of it.

Unexpectedly, though, when she was certain that the next sound she would hear would be Lyle Hetherington slamming out of her flat, she heard no such sound. But, to her tremendous surprise, the next sound she heard was Lyle Hetherington walking over to where she stood.

'You sound—fed up,' he commented, and his voice was neither angry nor icy now.

'That's an understatement,' she answered without turning.

'No other men friends?' he queried, and at that Kelsa did turn round.

'Look,' she snapped, 'and for the *last* time, your father was *never* a man friend to me in that sense.' She would have turned her back on him again but, crazily, she again remembered Lyle Hetherington's brunette companion of two weeks ago, and all at once it seemed a point of honour that she tell him. 'But of course, I've got *other* men friends—I'm not a nun.'

'But you are a virgin!' he tossed back at her sharply before she could blink.

Kelsa sighed. She was never going to win, not with him! 'And not a very wise one at that,' she lobbed back, tired suddenly of having to defend herself to this man. 'I've thought and thought until my head hurts to try and understand why your father should have left me half of everything in his will.' She paused, then challenged, 'They say two heads are better than one—why don't *you* try and work it out?'

'If I take everything you've said as gospel, you mean?'

'I refuse, categorically refuse,' she flared, 'to repeat that never at any time was I your father's mistress.'

'You just did,' Lyle replied, and, after giving her a long level stare, he walked over to the door. It was from his stance by the door, however, to her amazement, he commented quietly, 'I'll see what I can do,' and went.

Some hours later Kelsa went to bed, and was still trying to take in the fact that, from Lyle Hetherington's parting remark, there seemed to be a hint that he might now be prepared to believe her. There was a smile on her lips as she closed her eyes.

CHAPTER SIX

WITHOUT knowing it, Kelsa was singing in her shower the next morning. She was still singing a snatch of a tune when, while drying herself, she realised she felt much happier than she had recently. She even felt hungry.

Tucking into a couple of slices of toast and marmalade, she thought over Lyle Hetherington's visit the previous evening. Then she realised she felt quite heartened that Lyle was perhaps at last ready to change his mind about her, and might perhaps be more receptive to believing that maybe she wasn't quite so scarlet as he would have her painted. He'd more or less promised to help her find out why his father had left matters the way he had, anyhow, so things were decidedly looking up.

In fact, Kelsa thought when even her car started at the first attempt, everything seemed much brighter this morning. She was fifteen minutes ahead of schedule for the office too, so all augured well for her to get some work done before the phones started ringing.

Feeling in a far more cheerful frame of mind than she had been of late, Mr Hetherington's death having given cause for much sadness, she made her way along the corridors to her office. It was Lyle Hetherington who was in her thoughts as she opened her office door, though. Lyle, and the fact that he had shown signs of being disposed to believe her.

In the next two seconds, however, she discovered that she had been living in a fool's paradise if she believed that. For, just leaving his father's old office, and striding towards her, his face a chiselled mask, was Lyle.

'G——' The greeting died in her throat when, without a glance at her, without a word to her, but staring straight in front of him—and as if his visit to her flat last night had never been—Lyle reached the door and—strode straight out!

Feeling winded by what had happened in so few seconds, Kelsa stared at the empty doorway. With her breath sucked in from the shock of it, she slowly closed the door and collapsed on to her chair. And she had thought he might be on the way to changing his opinion of her!

She would like to have believed that Lyle, not so much cutting her dead but walking past as though in his view she did not exist, might have another interpretation than the obvious one. But she had fooled herself last night into thinking he might be starting to believe her. She wouldn't fool herself again. He had every right to be in his father's office—more right than any of them. But while some sensitive part of her wanted to believe that perhaps, while stopping off to pick up something he needed from his father's office, maybe, with his father's death so recent, Lyle's emotions had caught at him and left him a little ragged, she was sure it wasn't that. Quite plainly Lyle Hetherington was regretting having given her a moment's credence, and was loathing her with renewed vigour this morning.

Kelsa wished she could be angry about it, but she couldn't. Instead she felt strangely hurt and vulnerable where he was concerned, somehow.

Having gone in a little early to have a head start on the day, she discovered she had done precisely nothing by the time Nadine arrived. 'Everything all right in your corner?' asked Nadine.

'Fine,' Kelsa brought herself up short to find a smile.

'You've got a sort of pensive look in your eyes,' Nadine commented.

'I've a lot to think about these days.'

'Well, if you need another head, you've only to ask,' Nadine volunteered.

'Thanks, Nadine,' said Kelsa, but felt there wasn't much she could confide, or get her help with either, for that matter, that Nadine didn't already know about. For Nadine knew more than most about how Garwood Hetherington had left her so much, and how his son was far from ecstatic about it. And if Nadine had any idea at all why Mr Hetherington had mentioned her in his will at all—without there being such a colossal amount involved—then Kelsa was certain that Nadine would have told her by now.

She and Nadine got down to some work and were still finding plenty to do when, at half past twelve, Lyle's PA came in for some work which Ramsey Ford had left with Nadine the day before.

'Lyle wants to look at it before the meeting this afternoon,' Ottilie Miller explained.

'Busy?' Nadine enquired.

'Up to my eyes. Though thank goodness Lyle was out for a few hours first thing! That gave me a chance to get the papers he wants for this afternoon ready.'

And while Kelsa was wondering if Lyle had gone straight from the building after she'd seen him first thing, or if he'd gone to his office and then gone somewhere on business, Nadine was commenting, 'Sounds like heavy stuff.'

'What can I tell you?' Ottilie responded. 'Lyle's so determined that if he has to beg, borrow or steal to finance his plans he'll do it.' With that she picked up the papers she had come for, and went on her way.

'So the meeting this afternoon must be about—er—Lyle's diversification plans,' Kelsa suggested to Nadine—who smiled and commented,

'You're learning!'

'And the business Lyle would be on first thing would be to see bankers, finance experts, and the like?'

'Keep that up, and you'll be doing my job,' Nadine grinned.

Kelsa went home after work that day feeling more unsettled than she had ever felt in her life. Nadine's remark about her doing her job came back to her as she fixed herself a light meal. With the chairman's job now open, there were rumours of a general shuffle round of top executives. And while it was certain that Lyle would be the new chairman, Nadine wasn't saying if she had been offered a move on to a higher job than she had now—leaving her seat free for Ottilie Miller—or what her plans were. But, as Kelsa daydreamed about her and not Ottilie Miller's being offered the job of PA to the chairman, excitement started to tingle in her. To see Lyle every day...

With the abruptness of having a bucket of cold water thrown over her, Kelsa rocketed out of her daydream. She knew without pretension that she was just not experienced enough to be offered the job of PA to the chairman. But as if she wanted it! As if she wanted to see *him* every day! She must be going crazy! This worry about his father's leaving her such a legacy must be getting to her. Heavens, she didn't even like Lyle Hetherington!

In no time Kelsa pulled herself together. It was certain he did not like her. Nor would he want to see her every day. For that matter, it would probably make him delirious with joy if he never had to see her again.

Having sorted that out, Kelsa ate her meal, then washed up. While she was deciding what to do next, however, a ring sounded at her doorbell.

Expecting it might be one of her neighbours, she went and answered the door—then discovered, as her heart gave a crazy flutter, that for some reason Lyle Hetherington must want to see her again. For it was he, his face the same mask of concealed emotions it had been that morning, who stood there.

He looks tired, she couldn't help thinking, and knew he must have had a difficult meeting that afternoon. Had he found time to have anything to eat? she wondered. But when she realised she was thinking in terms of offering to get him something, so, at his dark frown that she wasn't inviting him in, she realised she was going to have to toughen up.

'If you've come to re-endorse your belief that I was your father's mistress, then I've heard it all before!' she snapped for starters, knowing from his grim expression that she could forget all pleasantries.

'I haven't!' he clipped.

'You—haven't?' Staring at him, she saw a muscle come alive in his temple, and suddenly, with a touch of the same empathy she'd sometimes felt with his father, she realised that Lyle was exceedingly tense about something. 'You'd better come in,' she invited at last, as she realised that if he hadn't called to have another go at her about her being his father's mistress, then since his meeting that afternoon had been so tough, he must be here to insist on her reassurance that she would not milk the company. 'Will you be staying long?' she asked as she squared up to him in the centre of her sitting-room carpet.

'I want a lot of answers!' he grated, and stepped back from her for all the world as though she was tainted, and he didn't want to stand too close.

And that, Kelsa suddenly found, was hurtful to her. For two pins, though, as pride gave her a nudge, she would have told him that in her view he already had her word that she wouldn't touch a penny until she knew why his father had made her a beneficiary of his will.

But, as her pride dipped, and her conflicting heart softened because he'd had such an uphill day, 'Take a seat,' she bade him coolly, indicating the settee, and, turning her back on him, she went over to the chair she had sat in the previous evening. 'So,' she began coldly, as she determined to be every bit as tough as he was as, taut-jawed, he sat opposite her, 'you haven't come here to again accuse me of being your father's——'

'I said not!' he cut her off aggressively—but added, to her total astonishment, though still in the same aggressive manner, 'I now know that you and he were not lovers! I now have proof.'

All the coldness which she had been at pains to show him abruptly vanished, and for a moment she stared open-mouthed. 'You—do?' she gasped. 'You have?' she asked, confused because when he should be smiling and happy to know that, he was looking nothing of the kind. 'How?' she had to ask then, the question being quite a natural one, she would have thought as she wondered how, when *she* couldn't prove it, *he* could!

His answer, though, left her as baffled as before, since it was no answer at all, but a tightly gritted and accusing, 'Why didn't you tell me?'

'*Tell you*?' Kelsa exclaimed, suddenly growing furious with this man who had never believed a word she had said, and was now laying a charge of withholding facts which she had repeated again and again to him. 'Heavens above,' she stormed, 'I *tried* to tell you! Till I was blue in the *face* I *tried* to tell you that your father and I weren't...'

'Not *that*!' he snarled, as ever unceremoniously chopping her off.

'What, then?' she flared, getting just the tiniest bit fed up with him. 'If not *that—what*?'

'You're maintaining that you don't know?' he challenged, and Kelsa could see that his temper was fraying severely around the edges.

'I'm lost,' she confessed—and that wasn't right either.

'Like hell you're lost!' roared Lyle, making no concession to her look of mystification.

'I haven't a clue what you're talking about!'

'Much!' he scorned, the fire of fury burning fierce in his grey eyes. 'It was just coincidence that you came to work at Hetheringtons, was it?'

Feeling absolutely baffled at what he was talking about, Kelsa stared at him through ever widening bright blue eyes. 'Well, I don't know what coincidence there is about it. I was living in Herefordshire when...'

'Not Warwickshire?' he cut in.

'My mother came from Warwickshire, I was——'

'I know she came from Warwickshire,' he growled. 'I've——'

'How on earth do you know that?' Kelsa cut him off for a change. 'I know I mentioned to your father that my mother came from a place called Inchborough, but I wouldn't have thought he'd have been interested enough in that snippet to pass it...'

'*Interested*! *Ye gods, he*...' suddenly, it was as if Lyle was under some kind of pressure beyond bearing, for all at once he shot to his feet, and, while still keeping his distance but with his tone more controlled, everything about him seeming to be being held in stern check, 'Why didn't you tell me,' he began, quietly this time, and looking directly into her eyes, 'that you——' he paused '—are my sister?'

'*Sister*?' she gasped, her reply instant, automatic, and utterly flabbergasted.

She was still staring witlessly at him when he revealed succinctly, 'My father originated from Inchborough too.'

'Did he?' she exclaimed, positively gaping. 'He didn't say anything about that when I told him that my mother came from there!' she said in surprise. But, as she started to get her thoughts back together again from the earlier astounding statement he had made, 'Well, that *still* doesn't make me your sister! Why, it's quite ridiculous,' she began to assert, but got no further.

'Ridiculous, is it?' Lyle cut in with the ease of a master. And before Kelsa could tell him that yes, it jolly well was, he was asking curtly, 'What was your mother's name before it became Stevens?'

She could hardly see the relevance, but, 'Whitcombe,' she replied, and in the trick of the light thought Lyle had lost some of his colour. 'Her maiden name was Whitcombe, but...'

'Then you *are* my sister,' he stated.

'How do you make *that* out?' she exclaimed, and, trying to understand Lyle's reasoning, saw that it somehow stemmed from his claiming to have proof that she wasn't his father's mistress. 'This proof you have that I wasn't having an affair with your father must lie in the fact that for some cockeyed reason, and based solely on the coincidence that your father and my mother came from the same town, you think I was—am—your father's daughter. What then?' she wanted to know, and quickly, as it struck her as quite odd that when she'd told Mr Hetherington that her mother came from Inchborough he had not said that so had he! 'You can't surely add that fact to the one that, having bumped into your father...'

'You told him your name—and were straight away promoted to his office,' Lyle Hetherington finished for her.

'That still doesn't make him my father!' she insisted. Somehow she didn't want Lyle for a brother. 'Frank Stevens was my father,' she stated firmly, 'and you'd have to go a long way to prove otherwise.'

'Oh, I can prove it,' Lyle retorted toughly, still on his feet, still keeping his distance from her as though fearing contamination.

'Go on, then,' she challenged, 'where is this proof? Where and when did you find it?'

'The proof is with me. It came from a locked drawer in my father's desk this morning.'

'This morning? You were leaving your father's office as I came in...'

'Right,' he nodded, and unbent sufficiently to explain, 'Ramsey Ford mentioned to me yesterday that there was a locked drawer in my father's desk which he couldn't find a key to. This morning, on my way to my own office, I went round with my father's keys to check before I handed that desk key to Ramsey that there was nothing private and personal in that drawer.' Lyle halted, and inserting a hand inside his jacket pocket, 'I found something very private—and personal,' he said curtly, and withdrew a folded piece of paper. 'I found this,' he stated heavily, going on, 'While it answers a lot of questions, it throws up a hell of a lot more.'

'What is it?' asked Kelsa.

'A birth certificate for a girl child, named Kelsa Primrose March.'

'My names!' she gasped.

'A girl child born to March Whitcombe and Garwood David Hetherington,' Lyle went on.

'*No*!' she exclaimed, so totally shocked that she felt her colour drain away.

A fact witnessed by the hard-eyed man facing her, for suddenly his tone had changed. 'Are you all right?' he asked in some concern. 'You look as if you're about to faint.'

She shook her head, and pushed through waves of faintness. 'I'm OK,' she murmured. 'A bit shaken, but...'

'Didn't you know?'

'It's not true!' she denied. 'My father was...'

'I'm—sorry,' seemed to be dragged from him, 'but it is,' and, moving closer to her, he opened out the certificate and handed it to her.

Kelsa took the piece of paper from him, but it was a second or two before, the words dancing before her eyes, she was able to make out that on the seventh of December, at Inchborough General Hospital, a girl child named Kelsa Primrose March had been born to March Whitcombe. The child's father, as Lyle had said, was Garwood David Hetherington.

'I can't believe it!' she whispered, still in shock.

'No more could I,' said Lyle. 'But there's no mistake. According to that document, my father went personally to register your birth. Not only has he stated to the Registrar that he's the father, he's also given the address he then lived at—the address where he and my mother lived before he bought their present home.' Whether he was thinking of his mother and how her husband had strayed and had an affair—had, while living with her, betrayed her—Kelsa didn't know, but a note of toughness had entered Lyle's voice when he questioned, 'You'd no idea?'

'Absolutely none!' she replied, staggered—and felt such an explosion of conflicting emotions inside her that all she was capable of doing was to stare down at the certificate in her hands. All was silent in her flat then as Lyle Hetherington, perhaps because he had witnessed the shock he had given her, stayed quiet as if to allow it all to sink in. Kelsa was still sitting stunned, though, her eyes on the certificate in her hands, when suddenly she declared stoutly, 'He wasn't!'

'Who wasn't?' Lyle challenged, looking at her as though she had suddenly gone off her head.

'Your father—he wasn't my father!'

'Hell's teeth, how much *more* proof do you want than *that* certificate!' Lyle ground out harshly.

'But it's not mine!' she exclaimed, and when he looked askance, 'It's not my birth certificate.'

'You're not Kelsa Primrose March——'

'I am, but my birthday's on the fourth of December, and——'

'There could have been a mistake.'

'And the year's wrong! I'm twenty-two. This Kelsa Primrose March is twenty-four,' she said, and as Lyle came and took the certificate from her, 'And I wasn't born in Inchborough,' she declared, not wondering, after the colossal shock she'd suffered, why she had been so slow to realise how wrong that certificate was. 'I wasn't born in hospital, but at my parents' home in Drifton Edge, Herefordshire.' Lyle switched his stern gaze from the certificate to her, his serious expression clearly doubting what she was saying. 'And *I*,' she told him, 'can prove it.'

'You can?' he questioned, his tone oddly strained, she felt.

'I can.'

'Then *do* so!' he rapped.

Kelsa was already out of her chair and on her way to the writing desk without his command. 'I'd no idea, none whatsoever, that my mother and your father so much as knew each other, much less that they were friends,' she added as she opened the lowest drawer. 'He never——'

'Lovers!' Lyle interrupted bluntly. 'They were lovers.'

'Lovers they may have been,' she had to agree, 'but...' she took out an envelope and then closed the drawer '...this says who my father really was.'

She got no further, because Lyle Hetherington, ever a man of impatience, it seemed, didn't wait for her to take the certificate from its envelope but taking the envelope out of her hands, did that job himself.

'You see!' she pointed out, stretching her arm over his and indicating the section she was reading. 'Place where born—my home in Drifton Edge—*and* note the date. A date of birth two years after the date on the certificate you have. Mother's name, the same March Whitcombe, but father's name Frank Thomas Stevens. I've even got their marriage certificate if you want to see it.'

'It has no relevance,' Lyle said crisply, but somehow, for all his short tone, Kelsa, her sensitivities suddenly working overtime, felt that he seemed, while still tense, a degree or two less strained than he had been. She was aware that, although he could read quite well without her help, shock was causing her to gabble on. Then she realised there was more physical evidence too, apart from her lost colour, of how she was feeling. 'Your hand is shaking,' Lyle declared suddenly—and Kelsa swiftly dug both her hands into the pockets of her jeans.

'You've delivered something of a bombshell,' she owned, having recovered from briefly believing that Lyle might be her brother to cope with the fresh shock of realising that her saintly mother had once had an affair—

and with a married man. 'I never knew that my mother had had another child.'

Lyle's look seemed to soften. 'Have you any brandy?' he asked.

'You'd like a drink?'

'For you, nut!' he told her, and for the first time since she had known him he smiled at her.

'Er—I don't have any,' she replied, and felt quite peculiar inside for a few moments. 'Um—would you like a coffee?' she asked.

'I'll make it,' he said straight away, and to her astonishment put some more space between them as he left her to go and take liberties with her kitchen.

By the time he came back Kelsa had subsided on to the settee, her head a quagmire of bitty recollections and thoughts. 'This isn't coffee—it's tea!' she exclaimed after the first sip from the cup he handed her.

'Said to be good for shock,' he informed her solemnly, and coming to sit beside her with his own cup. 'How are you feeling now?'

'Pretty staggered,' she had to confess, and felt such an empathy with him then, it was as if there had never been a time when she could have hit him, nor a time when it seemed he might throttle her. 'Little things keep coming back to me. Things I paid no heed to then, but which now that I know—about your father thinking I was his daughter, I mean—take on some meaning.'

'Such as?' Lyle prompted.

'Oh—such as my first meeting with him. I resemble my mother very strongly,' Kelsa inserted, 'and I realise now that your father probably spotted my resemblance to her straight away. He mentioned my smile, which is like hers, and then asked me my name.'

'You told him Kelsa Primr...'

'No, I wouldn't do that! That is, I said I was Kelsa Stevens, and he remarked that my name was unusual, and asked if I had any others.'

'It's a wonder he didn't have a heart attack then when you told him,' Lyle commented quietly.

'You do believe it was a coincidence, my coming to work at Hetheringtons? I didn't know about your father and my mother, honestly I didn't.'

'That's obvious,' said Lyle. The evidence was there before him, in the look of her. 'You're pale and trembling still from what I threw at you. But go on. You told my father you were named Kelsa Primrose March—how did he react?'

'He suggested, from my third name, that perhaps I was born in March.'

'Lord, he could be a cunning devil when it suited him!' Lyle commented. 'You told him you were born in December, of course.'

Kelsa nodded. 'And also that I was named March after my mother.'

'And in a very few minutes he'd got it all. And the next *you* knew was that you were transferred from the Transport section to his office.'

'I *am* good at my job,' Kelsa felt she should make clear. But she also felt she had to confess, 'Though it was only on Friday that Nadine Anderson divulged how your father had told her I was to have the job regardless of whether or not I shaped up when she interviewed me.'

'It's clear, isn't it, that having—for whatever reasons—been deprived of knowing his daughter Kelsa all these years, he wanted her where he could see her daily, and get to know her.'

Kelsa realised that Lyle was probably right about that. 'But why didn't he ever say anything to me about thinking I was his daughter?' she just had to question.

'Who can tell?' Lyle shrugged. 'Any number of options are open. He could well have thought you knew you were his, but had been legally adopted by Frank Stevens. Or maybe he thought you didn't know—but, for whatever reason, had never seen a copy of your original birth certificate. But whatever he believed on that score, I can see now that he planned very shortly to either tell the world about you, or, at the very least, tell me that I had a sister.'

'Oh, I remember now—your father wanted to tell you something personal as soon as you got back from Australia.'

'Bright girl!' Lyle smiled. 'Only I—we never managed to find time for that private talk.'

'I'm sorry,' Kelsa murmured sensitively, but couldn't help adding, 'Oh, why didn't he double-check everything?'

'Why would he?' Lyle replied. 'Everything was there. He had your name, the fact that you were born in December, the fact that your mother's name was March, and the fact that she came from Inchborough—what was there to double-check? Add the fact that you resemble your mother, and——'

'Oh, I've just remembered,' Kelsa butted in. 'That night—the night he gave me a lift and came in to make a forgotten phone call. Well,' she went on, aware now, as Lyle looked back at her with friendlier grey eyes than she was used to, that, while it was conceivable his father had used that phone call as a ruse, Lyle no longer doubted that there had been a phone call to be made, 'we somehow got talking about my parents, and he said he was glad when I told him we were a very happy family. Anyhow, he then remarked that I hadn't a photo of my parents around, so I showed him one of my mother and father—and he said I was exactly like my mother in looks.'

'So, having seen for himself the final endorsement that the woman who gave you birth was the same woman who gave birth to his Kelsa Primrose March, what more was there for him to check on?'

Only the *exact* date of her birth, Kelsa realised. But he hadn't and—it was all so traumatic. She was still feeling very much shaken, she had to admit. And it seemed that she and Lyle Hetherington between them had examined as much as they knew in detail, but it wasn't enough.

'You're still upset?' he observed quietly, his glance on her pale face.

'I want—*need*—to know more.'

'There are some questions unanswered,' he agreed, and getting straight down to basics, 'You spoke of your mother in the past tense.'

'She's dead,' Kelsa replied flatly.

'Any chance you could ask your father to fill in the blanks? There's a hope he may know...'

'He died with my mother. They were in a hire car, in an accident two years ago while holidaying in Greece.'

'Poor Kelsa,' Lyle said softly, and touched her hand in a moment of sympathy.

But even as her skin tingled at his touch he was pulling his hand back and getting up from the settee. There was a restless kind of look about him, she noticed, as he carried the tray with the used teacups on back to the kitchen.

By the time he was back, though, she had recovered from the unexpectedness of his touch. 'Would *your* mother know, do you think?' she asked.

'Knowing my father, I'd say it would be most unlikely that he'd confess to any extra-marital affair unless he had to. But, even if she does know, I'm afraid I don't feel that at this particular time it's quite the moment to rekindle what would be an old wound.'

'You're right, of course,' Kelsa instantly agreed. 'I'm not thinking straight yet or I'd never have suggested such a thing,' she apologised, and tried to think logically. 'I've never been to Inchborough, but I can see now it's the only place to start,' she announced.

'You're going to go to Inchborough?'

'If I can find someone who lived there at the same time as my mother, I can...' She broke off, something in Lyle's expression telling her that he had just thought of something. 'What is it?' she asked urgently.

'My aunt—Aunt Alicia. She was born and brought up in Inchborough.'

'Do you think she might know something?' Kelsa questioned eagerly.

'She might,' Lyle murmured thoughtfully. 'I have to say, though, that it's doubtful. There was about a twenty-year gap between her and my father, and he left the family home soon after she came on the scene. Though I suppose it's possible she might have heard if there was any gossip going around. Come to think of it,' he remembered suddenly, 'I seem to recall that she looked quite shaken to see you at Burton and Bowett's last Wednesday. I was too enraged to give thought to it at the time, but—I wonder?'

Kelsa had forgotten nothing about Lyle's fury that day. But she had other priorities just at this moment. 'C-could you try her tonight? Telephone her...'

'It—seems important to you?' Lyle looked into her beautiful blue eyes to question.

Kelsa looked away. It was rare for her to confide her innermost feelings to anyone, but—and quite astonishingly given his previous record—she had a feeling that

Lyle would understand as she revealed quietly, 'I've—sometimes been a little lonely since losing my parents. I've no other relatives, but h-having just discovered I have a sister somewhere, and although she must have been adopted and will probably be known by another name—I just *have* to find her.'

'Oh, Kelsa!' Lyle murmured, and with breathtaking gentleness he lightly touched his lips to her brow. Immediately, however, he drew back to ask, 'Where's your phone?'

Kelsa sat pale and anxious while, having initially to find his aunt's Essex telephone number, Lyle first contacted Directory Enquiries. Shortly afterwards he was busy dialling again—but the longer he stood with the phone against his left ear, the more certain she was that his call was unsuccessful.

'No reply,' he confirmed as he replaced the receiver, and, at her crestfallen expression, 'Not to worry, she won't always be out.'

'It was good of you to try,' she thanked him politely, and realised when after a moment or two he took a step towards the door that there was little more to say.

'You'll be all right if I go now?' he enquired.

'Grief, yes,' she lied.

'I'll be in touch,' he stated.

'Goodnight, Lyle,' she smiled, and went to the door with him.

'Goodnight,' he nodded, and went quickly, while Kelsa went back to the settee.

She stayed there for some hours—indeed, she saw little sense in going to bed. For how was she going to sleep? She had a half-sister out there somewhere. And Lyle—Lyle Hetherington wasn't always the swine she had dubbed him. In fact, once they had sorted out that she wasn't his sister, and that nor had she known that his father had believed she was, Lyle had shown a much more sensitive and super side to his nature. In actual fact, he had been rather wonderful.

Realising that she wouldn't be fit for work in the morning if she didn't get some rest, Kelsa went to bed around midnight, to lie there wide-awake and excited. Though, with the many and varied thoughts that flitted in and out of her head that night, not once did she find the answer to why, when she so dearly wanted to find her sister, she did not want to have Lyle for a brother.

CHAPTER SEVEN

KELSA had barely slept, but lack of sleep was not the reason why, seated behind her desk the following morning, she was finding it so difficult to concentrate on her work. Her head was still spinning from the staggering information Lyle had acquainted her with last night!

It seemed incredible that she had a sister she had never known about. Had she, the other Kelsa, tried to find her family? she couldn't help wondering. It was a sensitive area, of course, if she too had been left in ignorance, or—a dreadful thought struck her—what if she didn't want to be found?

But she must! If she was anything at all like their beautiful mother, she would be warm and loving, and... Kelsa's thoughts flitted on to her mother, as they frequently had since Lyle's visit. Her poor dear mother—there was so much she wanted to know. How had she broken up with Garwood Hetherington? Had it been her decision or his? It went without saying, whatever the answer to these questions, that she must have suffered over it, for no one gave up their baby for adoption without knowing a great deal of pain.

Was that why her mother had brought her up so strictly—to safeguard her? Because she, aware of life's pitfalls, didn't want her to know any of the harrowing feelings she must have lived with.

With her thoughts swinging from her mother to her need to find her sister, and on to Garwood Hetherington, Kelsa realised that her half-sister would be Lyle's half-sister too. Not that he seemed too thrilled to have a sister, she mused as she recalled that his attitude last night had definitely been anti until she'd proved to him that they were not related.

Which, she suddenly realised, made Lyle quite a nice person. Because, though he could have little interest in finding his half-sister himself, he had put himself out last night to try and contact his aunt—when he'd seen that, shocked and shaken though she might be, she was determined to find her elder sister.

Would he, as he'd said, be in touch? Or would he this morning have thought better of trying to contact his aunt to see if she knew anything?

Half an hour later, at about ten-thirty, when the internal phone on her desk rang, Kelsa had her answer. 'Kelsa?' Lyle's deep-timbred voice set her nerves jangling.

'Yes,' she confirmed huskily.

'I've managed to contact my aunt.'

'And?' she questioned eagerly, nervously, before he could continue.

'And we'll go and see her.'

'*We*?' she questioned, starting to feel shaky again inside, for *surely*, for Lyle to be thinking of going to see his aunt, *and* taking her with him, it meant that Mrs Ecclestone *must* know something.

'I've a loaded schedule,' Lyle went on, that 'we' an established fact, apparently, 'but I can take a couple of hours off this afternoon. How about you?'

This afternoon! Things were moving fast—and Kelsa, realising that Lyle wasn't a man to drag his heels, swiftly bucked her ideas up. 'This is important enough for me to find time,' she told him as calmly as she could.

'Two o'clock, then,' he said, and rang off.

Kelsa shakily put her phone down, and guessed she must be looking a little strained, for when she glanced at Nadine she saw that the older woman was looking at her in some concern.

'I'm all right,' Kelsa assured her quickly, and hurried on, 'Th-that was Lyle. There's—some important business that's come up which he and I are going to—um—look into this afternoon.' She swallowed, then asked, 'OK with you if I have the time off?'

For a solemn moment or two Nadine surveyed her face, noting that her colour was returning. Then suddenly a grin spread across her face. 'You're the boss!' she reminded her.

And, as Kelsa got back down to some work, it also reminded her that she now had the answer to that question that had plagued her when considering that Garwood Hetherington never did anything without a reason. For while, of course, she was not the boss, it was now quite clear that that dear man had only left her so well provided for because he believed she was his daughter. Since, though, it was equally clear that she was not his daughter, she would naturally give up all claim to that inheritance.

For quite a few seconds Kelsa reflected on the empathy she had occasionally shared with Garwood Hetherington. Could it be the fact that she was her mother's daughter, perhaps somehow had her mother's ways, that was responsible for that empathy, that sensitivity she had felt towards him? For some unknown reason then, Kelsa recalled the empathy, the sensitivity, which she had felt with Lyle last night. But, since being her mother's daughter didn't in any way explain anything where he was concerned, she gave it up.

Anyhow, there were far more important issues to be addressed here than empathy, or legacies. Lyle was taking her to see his aunt, Garwood Hetherington's sister, this afternoon, and...

Suddenly Kelsa fell to wondering if perhaps her own sister was married and had children of her own. A smile traced her mouth—oh, how marvellous, she could be an aunt herself for all she knew. She could have a nephew, or a niece—or both!

She was unable to eat a morsel at lunchtime, so she stayed in her office working. At twenty to two she went and washed her hands and, beset by nerves again, she suddenly realised that she had no idea if Lyle intended that she should meet him in the car park by his car, or where.

She had her topcoat on over her warm pink sweater and fine wool grey pleated skirt, and she bent to pick up her bag. It was about ten to two and she was just preparing to leave her office, however, when the office door opened and Lyle came in.

'Ready?' he queried, his grey eyes running over her shiny blonde head and superb skin.

For answer, she joined him at the door, and was a mass of jumpy emotions when, although tall herself, she seemed to come up only to his shoulder. Beside him she walked along the corridors, and stood beside him in the lift as it descended.

'Had anything to eat?' he enquired as they stopped by reception and the blushing young woman behind the desk handed over a paper bag.

'I couldn't,' Kelsa replied, and was sitting beside him in his Jaguar when he opened the bag and, sharing the spoils with her, passed a cellophane package over to her.

'Try,' he suggested, and started his car. Kelsa realised that he hadn't had time to have anything to eat yet.

'I'm sorry,' she could do no other than apologise, 'I'm putting you to an awful lot of trouble.'

'Hey——' he refused to allow that '—this concerns me too, you know.'

'Oh, I'm sorry,' she apologised for a second time. 'Kelsa's your sister too, I know, only...' Her voice trailed off. If he was interested in finding her after all, it didn't seem very polite to mention her earlier opinion that he wasn't.

'Eat a sandwich,' he instructed.

'That's as good a way as any of telling me to shut up,' she commented, but, glancing at him, was quite surprised, to see him grin.

There was little conversation for quite some minutes as Lyle steered his Jaguar in the direction of Essex. But Kelsa's anxieties were peaking again, and she could feel herself growing more and more tense. Soon she might know something!

'What did your aunt say—I mean, what did you say, when you rang her?' burst from her when her inner tension suddenly became too much for her.

'It wasn't much of a conversation,' Lyle replied, giving a sideways glance at her tense expression. 'Bearing in mind that we'd no idea if she knew your mother, I began by asking her if the name March Whitcombe meant anything to her.'

It obviously did, or she wouldn't be sitting beside him on their way to see her, Kelsa realised. 'What did she say?' she asked, striving to stay calm.

'She only had to say "I wondered if somebody might ask me that" for me to know that she might hold the key to a lot we want to know. She confirmed it when I followed on by telling her how March Whitcombe was now dead, but that I should like to come and see her and bring March Whitcombe's daughter with me.'

'She—didn't mind?' Kelsa asked quietly.

'She was upset that your mother had died—they'd been great friends at one time, apparently.'

'Really?' Kelsa questioned eagerly.

'So Aunt Alicia said. Anyhow, when I put it to her that you feel a need to have certain answers, she replied that she feels she owes it to you to fill in any blanks.'

Oh, heavens, Kelsa thought—this was far better than she could have hoped. A silence filled the car after that, though, and the nearer they got to Olney Priors where Mrs Ecclestone lived, Kelsa grew more and more inwardly churned up. Fill in any blanks! There were great gaping voids to be filled in!

Once they reached Olney Priors, the fact that brother and sister had not been close was made obvious by the fact that Lyle had to ask directions to his aunt's home. Clearly he had never been there. But in a matter of minutes he had found the address he was seeking, and pulled up outside a modest detached house.

Leaving the car, Kelsa walked with Lyle up the path to the front door and did her best to get on top of her emotions when Lyle, perhaps seeing the state she was in as they waited for the bell to be answered, caught hold of her hand and gave it a reassuring squeeze. Then the door was opening, and the fortyish lady whom Kelsa remembered seeing at the solicitors was warmly welcoming them in.

'I knew when I saw you, when I heard your name, who you were, my dear.' She shook hands with Kelsa, and, plainly taken by some emotion, she leaned forward and kissed Kelsa's cheek. Then, relieving Kelsa of her coat, she ushered them into the sitting-room. 'Can I get you some tea after your drive—the kettle is boiled already?' she offered.

'If you don't mind, Aunt Alicia, Kelsa really is most anxious to hear what you have to tell her,' Lyle declined for the two of them, and Kelsa shot him a grateful look.

'Shall we sit down, then?' Alicia Ecclestone smiled, and once they were all seated she looked to Kelsa and enquired, 'What is it you want to know? I'd be pleased to help in any way I can.'

'There isn't a lot I do know,' Kelsa explained, 'but Lyle said that you and my mother were friends, and——' she cleared her throat nervously '—and I wondered if you knew that my mother—had a baby—before she had me?'

'You don't know...? Your mother never told you about...?'

'It wasn't until last night, when I showed her the birth certificate I came across in my father's private papers, that Kelsa became aware that my father and her mother knew each other—much less that between them they'd produced a baby,' Lyle slotted in.

'Oh, good gracious!' his aunt exclaimed. 'It must have been a tremendous shock to you, Kelsa. You too, Lyle,' she suddenly realised.

'That's probably the understatement of the year,' he commented, but smiled.

'Oh, how like your father you are!' his aunt exclaimed. 'Not so much in looks, though you do feature the Hetheringtons. But your ways—I've followed your progress in the paper,' she confessed. 'Being at odds with your father all these years hasn't made me forget the young man you were—until I saw you at those solicitors' a week ago, I hadn't seen you for about sixteen years.'

'Kelsa's very like her mother, I believe,' Lyle brought her attention back to where he wanted it.

'She's the image of her. I'm sorry,' Alicia Ecclestone apologised to Kelsa, 'you're anxious to know all that happened in those days before you were born, and here am I, guilt-ridden that I never made it up with Garwood, when he was so generous as to remember me in his will.'

'That's all right,' Kelsa said quietly, and Lyle's aunt favoured her with a smile of gentleness, then seemed to gather herself together.

'I'll start at the beginning, I think, but just say if I'm going over anything you already know.'

'Fine, Aunt,' Lyle agreed, and, as intent as Kelsa, he listened as she went back twenty-five years.

'Um...' Alicia Ecclestone hesitated for a moment as if to know where to begin, then declared, 'Well, to fill in a little of the background—though if either of you find this too painful, do stop me.' She smiled before going on. 'Garwood and I came from a financially poor background. Though what my brother lacked in money he more than made up for in brains, shrewdness and drive.'

'He was always going to make it to the top,' Lyle inserted.

'Oh, there was never any doubt about that—he was one of life's winners from day one,' she agreed as if she'd always known it for a fact. 'He was nineteen when I was born, and according to my parents he was burning with ideas and ambition even then.' Her smile faded, and a sad look came into her eyes as she added solemnly, 'I saw for myself just how painfully ambitious he was when he later deserted my friend.'

'He deserted my mother?' Kelsa asked quickly as what Garwood Hetherington's sister had said unravelled in her brain.

'I'm afraid so,' she confirmed, but added, 'Though perhaps—although I didn't see it at the time—he didn't have too much of an option. But...' she paused, 'I'm overrunning events. I was still a toddler when Garwood left home, nor did it mean much to me that at twenty-one, having met an heiress, he married her.'

'My mother,' Lyle documented.

'Your mother,' she agreed. 'It was Edwina's money that gave him the financial backing he needed to start off the Hetherington Group, and——'

'Not to the full extent of the financing he required,' Lyle chipped in.

'You probably know more of the background than me there,' his aunt smiled, then stated, 'What I do know, because it later came to light when everything blew up with poor dear March, was that Edwina had a pretty shrewd head on her shoulders herself when it came to money.'

Startled, because from the sound of that it seemed as if Edwina Hetherington had known that her husband had strayed, Kelsa glanced swiftly from Mrs Ecclestone to Lyle. But if he was thinking the same there was nothing in his expression to show what he was thinking. But, his tone even, 'Go on, Aunt,' he prompted, 'you were saying how my mother agreed to give my father the money he...'

'In actual fact she didn't give it, but agreed to *advance* certain sums if your father could find a bank who would match it.'

'Which he did.'

'Which he did,' she agreed. 'And from then on your father worked all hours, so that it was a foregone conclusion that the business would prosper. But Garwood was still brimful of ideas and ambition, and set his sights on opening up another factory, a larger one this time. Which, by again borrowing heavily, he achieved.'

'That would be our Midlands plant.'

'That's the one. Anyhow,' she resumed, 'by the time I was seventeen things were a little easier financially at my home and I was able to go to secretarial college in Inchborough. You'd be about twelve years old then, Lyle, and were away at boarding school. Forgive me,' she broke off to apologise, 'but since your telephone call this morning, I've gone over and over everything in my head. With Kelsa saying just now that there isn't very much that she knows, I'm doing my best to put matters into a sequence of events.'

'You're doing fine, Aunt,' Lyle encouraged, and again she picked up her thread.

'We seldom saw anything of Garwood in Inchborough in those days. With him leaving home when I was so small, to me he was more a man who called once a year with Christmas presents than a brother. That Christmas of my seventeenth year, though, we had a friend of mine from secretarial college staying with us.'

'My mother,' Kelsa guessed, her insides churning once more as it seemed they were getting close to the point that she was eager to know about.

'Your mother,' Alicia agreed. 'Her parents, your grandparents, had her late in life, and were quite repressive in the way they brought March up. It seemed a miracle to both of us that they allowed her to come at all to stay with us for a whole week that Christmas, but they did.' She paused, then added, 'March was at my old home when my brother paid us his annual visit.'

'That's how they met,' Kelsa documented softly.

And Alicia Ecclestone sighed. 'She was seventeen, unworldly and beautiful. And Garwood, even though he was over twice her age, was married and had a son, took one look at her and immediately fell in love with her.'

'And—my mother?' Kelsa asked chokily.

'She was swept off her feet! She didn't know men, had never been allowed a boyfriend. Quite simply, she lost her head. That was the one and only Christmas that Garwood didn't just drop off the Christmas presents and spend as little time with us as he decently could before, having done his duty, he'd disappear until the next Christmas.'

'He stayed longer that time?' Kelsa questioned.

'He stayed quite some time. And returned. And, by the next Christmas, March had been delivered of a child.'

'My sister,' Kelsa murmured huskily.

But there must have been something in her voice, she realised, that gave away something of the emotion she felt to know she had a sister. Because Alicia Ecclestone, her voice softened with sadness, came swiftly in to reveal, 'I'm so sorry, my dear, but I have to tell you that the baby didn't survive.'

'*No*!' Kelsa exclaimed, not wanting to believe it. Not wanting to realise that her chance to find a family had been taken from her before she had barely begun.

'You know this for certain?' she heard Lyle question his aunt.

'She died aged four weeks. I know for certain, because I was the only one of the family to go to the baby's funeral,' Alicia answered him sadly.

Kelsa saw all her hopes evaporate to nothing, and could have cried. But somehow she managed to hold herself together. 'Mr Hetherington...' she began shakily, and fought hard to hold down her emotion at what Mrs Ecclestone had just said. Suddenly then, though, something that was quite obvious struck her all at once. 'I was going to ask if Mr Hetherington didn't go to the funeral, but of course he couldn't have, because he didn't know that the baby had died. Couldn't have done,' she went on, pushing her emotions to the back of her and working it out as she went on, 'because he would never otherwise, as he must have done, believed me to be that daughter.'

'No, he didn't know,' Alicia Ecclestone agreed. 'As I said, he fell in love with your mother...' She broke off to turn to Lyle. 'I'm sorry if this is painful to you to hear, but...'

'I'll cope,' he assured her levelly. 'I'd like to hear all of it.'

'Very well,' she accepted, and continued, 'I've overrun what I was saying again, but I'd no idea you thought the baby was...well, I thought it best to tell you quickly. But to get back... In what time Garwood could snatch from his home and his work—and he was slaving away by then to get his other factory going—he would drive to Inchborough to see March. By that time she'd moved out of her parents' home and into a bedsit. Then, in a very short space of time, she had to tell Garwood that she was pregnant.'

'How did he take it?' Kelsa wanted to know.

'From what I can gather, he was all set to get a divorce and marry her.'

'My mother—she knew about the affair—the baby?' Lyle questioned.

'She did,' his aunt confirmed. 'Garwood told her everything, including the fact that he thought it was the only decent thing he could do—March was penniless and was expecting his child.'

'At a guess, I'd say my mother didn't take that lying down,' Lyle opined.

'You're right, she didn't. Um—we can all be a degree or two unforgiving at times,' his aunt commented. 'Edwina was certainly possessive of you and your welfare, anyhow,' she told him. 'Nor did she waste any time whatever in reminding Garwood that he already had a wife and a child, and had duties to you both too, and that both *he* and his *new* family stood to be penniless if he insisted on going ahead with his plan.'

'She threatened to withdraw her financial support for his new venture?' Lyle guessed straight off.

'She had the power to make him bankrupt,' his aunt explained, and while Kelsa heard Lyle suck in his breath, 'and she would have used it,' she added. And in Kelsa's view, you couldn't get much more unforgiving than that!

'Which would have meant that everything my father had worked for all those years would go down,' Lyle put in thoughtfully.

'Precisely,' Alicia acknowledged. 'So what could he do?'

'He had to choose, by the sound of it.'

'It wasn't much of a choice. The woman he loved and their child and penury, against the business he had striven so hard to build, the woman he married, and the son he thought the world of. He saw March twice more once he'd made that choice, once to tell her of his decision, and once again when she was in hospital with the baby. As he saw it then, all he had to give the baby was his name.' She looked over at Kelsa. 'It was he who went to register the birth of Kelsa Primrose, the names your mother had chosen.'

'Not March?' Kelsa asked.

'To add your mother's name was his idea. As far as I know after that, he never again returned to Inchborough.'

'And the baby?' Kelsa questioned softly.

'She was such a lovely little thing,' Mrs Ecclestone replied gently, 'but delicate from the start. Your mother moved from Inchborough when the baby was three weeks old, and I helped her move into her new home in Tilsey—it's in Gloucestershire. The baby seemed to be doing all right, though, but less than a week later she was rushed into hospital.' She swallowed at what seemed a painful memory. 'It was a dreadful time. March was beside herself with worry. But the break with Garwood had been made and, proud as she always was—perhaps even a little bitter—she made me promise not to breathe a word to him about any of her troubles.'

'A promise which you kept to the end,' Lyle commented.

'I did. It was probably from my own feelings of guilt that it was through me that they had met that I felt so furious with him because he'd just dumped her, so when baby Kelsa died I vowed he would never know from me.'

'What did my mother do afterwards?' Kelsa wanted to know. Her mother's pain felt like her own pain just then.

'She couldn't seem to settle, and she left Tilsey to move to Drifton Edge in Herefordshire. And it was there,' said Alicia on a happier note, 'that she met and married Frank Stevens. By then I'd met John Ecclestone and, in the way of things, March and I lost touch. I knew, though, that she was expecting again—and could only be pleased for her.'

'They were happy together—my mother and father,' Kelsa, with fond memories of both her parents, felt she had to state. And, realising that she must have heard about all there was to know now, 'Thank you very much, Mrs Ecclestone, for re-living all this for me.'

'It was the very least I could do,' Alicia told her.

'My father never so much as had an inkling that his daughter hadn't survived?' Lyle asked.

'Not from me. And recent events seem to make it certain not from anyone else either. As you may know, when John and I married we moved to his home village, not far from here. Then my parents' health started to fail, so we found them a house nearby so I could keep an eye on them. The next time I saw the three of you after my wedding was at, first your grandfather's funeral, and then when your grandmother died.'

'I remember. I was about twenty then,' said Lyle.

'And made in the same mould as your father—you were certainly going to make it to the top too. But I digress,' Alicia smiled. 'Your father and I had nothing we wanted to say to each other, and were more like strangers than brother and sister. But it was at your grandmother's funeral that, finding myself in an isolated corner with your mother—and maybe because that funeral brought back memories of another—I found myself telling her that the little girl, Kelsa, had died.'

'So she knew too, but didn't tell my father?' Lyle said quietly.

'I knew she wouldn't, as she obviously disliked being reminded of the affair. I didn't doubt it when she told me, quite firmly, that since her marriage had settled down there would be no point in Garwood's knowing now. In her view—forgive me, Kelsa,' Alicia broke off to apologise in advance, 'Edwina said he'd forgotten that *that* woman ever existed.'

'Which clearly he hadn't,' Lyle interposed. 'It's my guess he knew Kelsa for her mother's daughter the moment he bumped into her at the Hetherington building.'

'Is that how you became acquainted with each other?' Alicia asked on a gasp, and Kelsa explained how it had come about and all that had followed. 'Garwood must have been knocked sideways when he heard your name,' Mrs Ecclestone took up as Kelsa came to an end. 'Apart from your resemblance to your mother, there was no doubt in my mind who you were either when I heard the solicitor say your name. I just knew that you were March's second daughter.'

'Would my mother have known it too?' Lyle asked what Kelsa realised would be a perfectly normal question.

'I would think so,' his aunt replied. 'She'd have picked up on the name Kelsa, and the name March too, I'm fairly certain. Add to that the fact that Garwood as good as left Kelsa half of what he owned, and that would seem to confirm it.'

'He only left me what he did because he thought I was his daughter—but I'm not,' Kelsa felt she should state there and then.

But Alicia Ecclestone smiled gently at her again. 'You're March's daughter, and Garwood certainly owed her—very much so. It's most apparent to me that he must have been nursing feelings of the deepest guilt all these years—and chose this way to try and make amends.'

But he didn't know he was going to die so soon, Kelsa thought, and again felt sad at his passing, and sad about all she had heard. In fact, she felt so down just then that she was grateful, when Mrs Ecclestone suggested perhaps they might like some refreshment now, that Lyle refused on her behalf as well as his own. 'We should be getting back,' he commented easily, and stood up.

'John will be sorry to have missed you—he'll be home from work soon,' said Alicia, as she retrieved Kelsa's coat and saw them to the door.

'Thank you, Mrs Ecclestone, for telling me—us—all you have,' Kelsa found a smile to accompany her words.

'Oh, dear child,' she answered, giving her a warm hug, 'I so wish I could have given you happier news.'

Kelsa was silent on the drive back. She had so much on her mind, but chiefly, having so wanted to find her sister, it was like being bereaved to know that she had died all those years ago.

She tried to pull herself out of her feeling of despondency as she realised how loved by her mother her sister must have been for her mother to have felt a need to call *her* by the same names. But that didn't do any good, because loving her first baby had brought her mother nothing but pain.

But her father had taken care of her mother, Kelsa mused solemnly, as she searched for something that might lift this flat feeling which she could not shift. Her parents had been close and loving, she recalled, and realised then that it was virtually certain that her father had known all there was to know about her mother's brief but tragic affair with Garwood Hetherington.

Kelsa was feeling her mother's pain as if it was her own. But still, even when she thought of how her mother had been deserted by the man she loved when—his wife being prepared to jerk the purse strings, apparently—he had abandoned her, Kelsa could not hate him. She had known him, and had grown fond of him—and it seemed nothing would alter that.

She remembered Garwood's wife, Lyle's mother, and how, aristocratic and imperious, she had demanded to know, 'Who is this woman?' Kelsa couldn't in all honesty say she had taken to the frosty-looking woman, but that didn't stop her from seeing that she hadn't been served too well in any of this either. She must have had a most unhappy time of it when her husband had fallen in love with someone else.

Lyle was driving in an area that was starting to be familiar to her, when Kelsa suddenly found that she was wondering—had Lyle's father never been in love with his mother to start with? And, remembering how he had parted from her mother when his wife, holding the purse strings, had given him an ultimatum, had Lyle's father married Edwina for her money?

Alicia Ecclestone hadn't exactly said so, though if she had any sensitivity at all—which she had—she wouldn't have in front of Lyle. But was that what she was saying, what she had meant with her talk of his ambition, his drive, when she had related how at twenty-one, having met an heiress, he had married her?

Kelsa's thoughts strayed away from Lyle's parents, and to him and how he might probably be angry at the hurt his father had caused his mother. Her thoughts, however, were sad, and on the sister she had lost, when she suddenly became aware that Lyle was pulling up outside her block of flats.

'I'm going back to the office!' she told him with a start.

'Correction—I am; you're not.'

'But——'

'But nothing,' Lyle cut her off. 'You're emotionally wrung out. Come on, now,' he ordered with quiet charm.

Kelsa had always felt that she liked being in charge of her own life, but she had to admit that it was not at all unpleasant to allow oneself to be quietly bossed around occasionally. It wasn't unpleasant either to have Lyle's considerate hand beneath her elbow as he escorted her into her building and up to the door of her flat.

'Will you be all right?' he asked kindly when, the door unlocked, he looked down at her and seemed to read in her shiny blue eyes that she was fighting a battle with a feeling of depression.

'Yes, of course,' she answered, and, feeling stupidly tearful, 'I'm being ridiculous,' she owned.

'No, you're not,' he denied softly, and went with her into her sitting-room. 'You wanted a sister, and you've just been deprived of one.'

'You've b-been deprived of one too,' she could not help but mention.

'Oh, little Kelsa,' he murmured, and taking her gently in his arms, 'I've other family,' he pointed out, and oh, so tenderly he placed a light kiss upon her mouth.

'Is—um—this supposed to make me feel better?' she asked, striving hard to control her emotions.

'Does it?' he asked, and she just loved his grin. Her answer was to pull out of his arms, and he let her go. 'OK now?' he questioned, and she knew he was ready to go.

'A little fragile around the edges, but otherwise intact,' she smiled. 'Thank you for taking me to see Mrs Ecclestone today,' she added.

'I think we both needed to know,' he replied quietly.

He had moved to the door, his back to her, when she called his name. He halted, and turned.

'What is it?' he helped her out when she seemed stuck for a moment to know how to go on.

'My mother...' she said '...she was good, and kind. She—was a lady.'

'What are you trying to say?'

Tears, unshed tears choked her throat. 'She—my mother—she wasn't a tart,' she told him solemnly, and for long seconds he just looked at her.

Then, 'I know,' he replied.

'You—know?'

He smiled then, and her heart thundered, especially when he said softly, 'How could she have been—and produced a daughter like you?'—and the next moment he had swung round, and was gone.

Kelsa sank down into her easy chair when the door closed after Lyle. She was still sitting there, stunned, an hour later. Because, without having time to analyse why she should suddenly feel so much happier at his parting words, she realised several other things at once. For surely, to have said what he had must mean that he not only no longer thought of her as some woman after all she could get, but that he—liked her a little? And she did hope, oh, so very much, that he liked her, because she, she knew now, was very much in love with him.

When Kelsa went to bed that night it was to lie there and wonder why she had at first been so shaken to realise what her feelings for Lyle were. It was obvious, surely, and had been from that first time he had kissed her, when she had responded with such unusual abandon, that there was something very special about him for her.

She later lay awake and came to terms with the fact that, after hoping so much to be able to find her sister, she now knew that there was no sister for her to find.

When thoughts of Lyle began to penetrate the sadness of her thoughts, though, Kelsa let him in. She knew, when at long last she fell asleep, that there was absolutely no mistake about what she felt for him.

Had she any thought, though, that she might awaken on Thursday to find she had imagined it, then that thought was immediately cancelled when he was in her thoughts even before she opened her eyes. And oh, how she loved him the more when because she'd left her car parked at Hetheringtons yesterday, she left her flat intending to catch a bus—and saw that her car was now magically parked in the parking area of the flats where she lived!

She drove to work with a huge grin on her face, because Lyle must have arranged for someone to drive it over and, with luck, she might see Lyle that day.

Luck *was* with her, for around ten o'clock that morning, while Nadine was closeted in the other office with Mr Ford, the outer door opened and, tall, dark-haired and immaculately suited, in strolled Lyle.

'How's it going?' he asked, coming over to her desk and perching on the corner of it.

'Fine,' she smiled, and even though she knew he hadn't come in especially to see her, her heart drummed nevertheless.

She saw his glance go from her eyes to her smiling mouth, and still had her eyes on him when those warm grey eyes met hers again. 'An apology from me is way overdue,' he then stated seriously. 'Are you going to forgive me, Kelsa, for all the evil things I've ever said to you?'

Evil things? They were as *nothing*! 'Of course,' she answered sedately.

'Then you'll let me take you to dinner this evening?' he questioned with smiling charm.

'Who could resist such an invitation!' she laughed, and while her heart raced—she was going out with him tonight, *she was going out with him*!—Lyle casually moved away from her desk.

'I'll call for you at eight,' he smiled, and just then the door between the two offices opened and Nadine came out, and as they exchanged greetings Ramsey Ford spotted Lyle through the open doorway.

'Ah, Lyle!' he called, 'I wanted to have a word. Any news of your plans for...'

'I'm working on it, Ramsey,' Lyle replied, and Kelsa was still watching him when, in a splendid humour, she saw, he walked into his father's old office. 'Last night I thought of one excellent way to secure the backing I need,' he was saying as the door closed on the two men. And that was when it struck Kelsa that she hadn't yet found time or space to tell Lyle that she didn't think she had any right to what his father had left her, nor did she want it, and that furthermore she intended to give up all claim to it.

But—her eyes grew dreamy and a smile touched her mouth—she'd have plenty of time and space to tell him tonight.

CHAPTER EIGHT

LYLE called for her at a few minutes before eight, but Kelsa was ready. In fact she had been as ready as she ever would be to see him again at half-past seven. Looking outwardly calm and serene in a smart deep salmon-coloured dress of fine wool crêpe, she smiled serenely as she opened the door to him, and hoped desperately, as she invited him in, that he had no idea of how fast her heart was racing just to see him.

'I'll just get my bag,' she murmured in pleasant, even tones, and almost had to drag her eyes from those warm grey eyes that, dared she hope, seemed to be admiring?

She walked without haste to her bedroom, but once there and away from Lyle's vision she swallowed hard. Realising that she was inwardly trembling, she picked up her small clutch-bag, but still had to take a few seconds out to try and pull herself together.

'Ready,' she stated lightly when she joined him again.

And having thought she'd pulled herself together, she promptly fell apart again when Lyle, delaying leaving her flat for a few moments, looked down into her bright blue eyes and complimented, 'Kelsa, you're lovely.'

'Why, thank you,' she somehow managed to reply, and as if she was used to receiving such wonderful compliments from him every day of the week. 'Thank you for getting my car to me, by the way. I forgot to mention it this morning.'

'My pleasure,' he murmured lightly, and escorted her from the flat to his car, and on to a smart but discreet kind of restaurant.

Dining out with Lyle ranked as one of the most marvellous experiences of her life, Kelsa decided. He was witty and charming, and she couldn't remember a time when she had ever thought him a monster. He was a man who knew his way around too, but at the same time asked her opinion on several of the issues they touched on—none of them business-related. Though probably because most of all he was the man she loved, the evening simply flew.

Kelsa had little idea of what she ate; all she knew was that Lyle seemed to be enjoying her company as much as she was enjoying his—and that made everything in her world perfect. 'We'll have our coffee in the annexe,' he told an attentive waiter, and it was with a start of surprise that Kelsa realised she had eaten her way through four courses and had barely realised it.

The annexe they adjourned to was a small alcove area off the large plush lounge. And Kelsa was further enchanted when, as they shared a couch, and their conversation for the first time touched on something around the office, that Lyle disclosed, 'It's the talk of the boardroom that my father seemed a more completely happy man in the last weeks of his life.'

'I only knew him for a short while myself,' Kelsa replied, highly sensitive to the fact that Lyle had been away in Australia for some of those last weeks of his father's life and must be feeling saddened by that fact, 'but to me, although he could get cross, like the rest of us, when the occasion demanded it, he otherwise always seemed happy to me.'

'I'd suggest, Kelsa, that he was never cross with you,' said Lyle. 'In fact, I'm certain he never was.'

Feeling a little puzzled to know what he was getting at, though from the friendly look in his warm grey eyes she was sure it was nothing she should get upset about,

'Well, no, as a matter of fact I can't say that I ever saw him irritated with me,' she owned. 'But...' having for the first time that evening lost him somewhere '...I don't think I understand what you're saying,' she had to confess.

'Sweet Kelsa,' he replied, and if that wasn't enough to make her heart thunder against her ribs, then the way his superb mouth lifted up at the corners in a gentle smile for her made it go into overdrive, 'haven't you realised yet what I've realised—that my father, contented and happy with his lot for the most part, had a corner, a part of him, that must have given him moments of regret and unhappiness.'

'My—m-mother, do you mean?' she asked tentatively, not wanting to upset him if Lyle was feeling a shade aggrieved about his own mother.

'My father, from what my aunt says—and I've no reason to disbelieve her—was given an ultimatum. But, although he abandoned your mother and his daughter, having made a conscious decision never to see either of them again, I just can't see my father, who was an honourable man in every other respect, honouring that decision without paying for it.'

'By—feeling unhappy about it?' Kelsa took a stab.

'Unhappy, and I'd say, while he learned to live with the decision he made, some small part of him was still missing—until he saw you in the corridors of...' Lyle broke off, then added, 'He may have got the wrong Kelsa, but I have you to thank, my dear, for the fact that once he'd learned that your mother was dead, because of his belief that you were his lost daughter, you were otherwise able to make his life complete, and completely happy.'

'Oh, Lyle,' Kelsa gasped, 'what a lovely thin[illegible] Thank you,' she added softly. He had al[illegible] gised for the dreadful things he had thought and said of her, and which she had freely forgiven. But what he had just said wiped out every last terrible accusation and word. But, striving to pull herself back together again lest Lyle should see something of how much his good opinion meant to her, 'It was such a coincidence, bumping into him in that corridor like that. I...'

'It was always on the cards from your first day in the building—or,' he commented as an afterthought, 'even in the car park.'

'Yes, I suppose so,' she acknowledged. 'Though it must have been fate at work all along, because it was never my intention, when I applied for a job at Hetheringtons, to move from Drifton Edge.'

'In Herefordshire,' he documented, and she smiled, purely because he had remembered where she came from. 'But,' Lyle went on, his eyes on the lovely curve of her mouth, 'whoever interviewed you spotted your potential, and offered you a job at head office.'

'I don't know about spotting my potential—I came up the hard way from the lowly transport section, remember.' She grinned saucily, and loved it when he laughed. 'Though it's true,' she owned, after another valiant attempt to control her hasty heartbeats and to not fall apart at the seams just because he had laughed at her attempts at humour, 'I was offered a plum job in another section—only I lost it because I was undecided what to do and dithered too long.'

'Why were you undecided?' Lyle asked, and, before she could answer, 'Boyfriend?' he enquired evenly.

'Oh, no,' she replied lightly, and as he waited for her to add more, 'I suppose it was just the fact that I'd been born in Drifton Edge, and grown up there, that it seemed a mammoth leap just to pack up and leave the place. Particularly as I had a house there.'

'You had a house there?' he pressed, and warmed her through and through by his apparent genuine interest.

'I still have it—it belonged to my parents,' she explained. 'I suppose some time soon I'm going to have to make some decision about it—whether to sell or let it,' she smiled. 'But in the meantime,' she ended, 'I go back to Drifton Edge most weekends, and . . .'

'Most weekends?' Lyle took up, and, his eyes narrowing slightly, 'You're sure you haven't some man friend tucked away in the wilds of Herefordshire?' he questioned.

'Positive!' she laughed, and for one crazy mixed-up moment thought he had sounded just the teeniest bit jealous, which just had to be so ridiculous that she dismissed it out of hand. 'I just go there to air the place, check that the pipes haven't frozen, perhaps take my favourite walk, see my friends . . .' Hoping she wasn't boring him out of his skull—though it was true he had that happy ability, she had discovered, of managing to look as if the smallest detail she imparted was of interest to him—she mentioned her closest friend Vonnie—how it had been Vonnie who had given her a nudge to find a more stimulating job than the one she had been doing.

'So we have your friend Vonnie to thank that we found you,' Lyle commented, and as her heart galloped, and her eyes stared, fascinated, at the wonderful upward curve of his wonderful, wonderful mouth, Kelsa knew that this wasn't merely one of the most marvellous experiences of her life, it was *the* most marvellous experience of her life. How could it be anything else? She was here, with the man she loved, and although she knew he must know lots of other, far more sophisticated women, just for tonight he seemed to be enjoying being with her.

That thought must still have been in her head, she realised when, their coffee finished, they left the restaurant and Lyle drove her back to her apartment. Because as he drew up outside her building, Kelsa knew she didn't want the evening to end, not just yet.

And even though they'd just had coffee, she pinned her hopes on the fact that Lyle too might want to extend the evening for a brief while, even if only for fifteen minutes. 'The coffee's instant, a bit of a comedown after what we've just had,' she turned to him to state in a rush, 'but you're welcome if you'd like...'

'I'd more than like,' she heard his superb voice, a smile in there somewhere in the darkness. 'I'll even go as far as to make it for you—how's that?' he offered.

Her heart leapt, joy filled her heart, even as, 'No, thanks,' she refused, 'your coffee tastes like tea!'

In shared laughter they went inside the apartment building and up to the door of her flat, where Lyle took her door key from her and undid the lock. Together they walked to the middle of her sitting-room. But as Kelsa halted and turned to him, intending to ask whether he wanted his coffee black or white, she looked straight into the warmth of his friendly grey eyes, and all at once what she had been going to ask went straight out of her head.

She was standing close to him, almost touching. And what he was reading in her glance she had no idea, but unhurriedly then he stretched out an arm and placed it around her shoulders, turning her that little bit more until they were standing closer still, but facing each other.

'You're beautiful,' he breathed, and giving her all the time in the world to back away if she felt so inclined, he gently pulled her against him.

But Kelsa did not feel in any way inclined to back away. 'Oh, Lyle,' she whispered, and, their two bodies in contact, she put her arms round him.

Gently he kissed her. Sweetly she returned his kiss. 'My dear,' he said on a breath of sound, and lowered his head once more.

His kiss that time was deeper, and Kelsa, her heart racing, her emotions already out of gear, leant against him as willingly she gave him her lips. She loved him when that kiss ended, and loved him more when he kissed her throat and held her safe to him.

In the firmness of his arms, in the security of his hold, she clutched on to him. She wanted to cry his name again, but his warm and wonderful mouth had captured hers again, this time with a greater degree of intensity. This time with such feeling that flames of wanting started to ignite and lick into a need that grew and grew.

Once more he kissed her, his hands caressing at her back. She felt his hands move down to her hips and pull her to him, heard a groan of wanting that left him, and, as her need for him spiralled, she just had to call out his name—'Lyle!'

Her body was on fire for his suddenly, and she pressed closer in her need for him—and heard a sound leave him, a sound that echoed the same aching need she was feeling.

'Sweet love,' he said deep in his throat, and with passion riding high, his mouth over hers, he moved with her, instinct somehow guiding him to her bedroom door. At her bedroom, he pulled back and looked into her eyes, his eyes asking a question.

But she loved him, and she wanted more. Her answer was to reach up and kiss him—and the next she knew they were through her bedroom door where, his jacket discarded somehow on the way, Lyle guided her to sit on her single bed.

To be closer still to him as he dispensed with his tie and she let her hands rove his shirt-covered back was bliss. But even more blissful was the way his hands caressed to her breasts, captured them and oh, so tenderly moulded them.

Quite when, without shame, she found that her dress had been unzipped and had been slipped from her, she had no idea. But, after a delightful kiss of wanting, of joy, she suddenly came to her senses, to realise that they were both now lying down on her bed, and that their top-clothes had disappeared.

But it wasn't shame but shyness, that caused her to bury her head in his hair-roughened chest. 'Are you all right, little one?' she heard him ask tenderly.

'Oh, Lyle,' she breathed huskily, and raising her head, their bodies so close on her narrow bed, so on fire, she wrapped her bare arms around him. 'Yes, I'm all right,' she smiled. 'Never better!'

They kissed then, and she felt his hands busy with the fastenings of her bra. 'I didn't think you went in for such contraptions,' he murmured as he expertly disposed of the bra, and to create yet more havoc inside her, his hands, warm and tender, caressed the silk creamy globes he had uncovered.

He bent his head to taste the joy in the hardened pink tips he had created, and, beside herself with need as his tongue caressed the pink pinnacle of her right breast, Kelsa vaguely realised he had been referring to how she hadn't had a bra on for him to remove the last time she had been in his arms. 'I'd been doing some washing... I mean... I'd... I always...' she came to a stammering halt, and actually felt herself blush at how gauche she sounded. Oh, grief, she worried, her only shame that he might realise just how naïve she was in this situation. She was ready to apologise, and even got as far as, 'I...' when just then Lyle stilled. Just then he ceased doing mind-bending things to her need-filled breasts.

Something was changing, she knew it was, when Lyle all at once somehow made some space and, looking down at her suddenly anxious expression, began, 'Tell me, Kelsa,' his voice gravelly, passion lurking there, she knew, 'that bit—about you being a virgin—is it true?'

'D-does it—show?' she asked, her voice breathless, shy—but never for a moment suspecting that her words would have the effect on Lyle that they did have. For to her wide-eyed amazement, and all in one movement, he suddenly swung his legs over the bed and, presenting her with his broad naked back, sat on the edge of the bed.

But, for all his firm tone, his breathing was ragged. 'Kelsa, girl, you're a bewitching creature, and a man could lose his head over you, but...' he began, but broke off, and seeming to make a gigantic effort, and gathering up his clothes as he went, he uttered the worst words she had heard all night. 'I'd better go.'

'G-go...?' she repeated, too stunned, too highly emotional then to conceal the fact that she didn't want him to go.

She knew he was serious, though. Even as part of her mind said that he couldn't seriously be thinking of going and leaving her like this, he was shrugging into his trousers, picking up his shirt.

He was halfway through her bedroom door when he turned, and from there told her quietly, 'I'm out of the country tomorrow for about a week,' then promised, 'I'll be in touch when I get back.' Then he was gone.

The sound of her apartment door closing was still ringing in her ears five minutes later, and still Kelsa was having a hard time in believing that—just like that—Lyle had gone.

It was around three in the morning when she eventually found a little rest from all the many worries that had presented themselves to her, chief among which was—why had Lyle stopped making love to her?

By the cold light of Friday morning, her sleep having only been fitful, Kelsa was certain she had the answer. She drove to her office knowing, beyond a shadow of a doubt, that Lyle *had* seen just how naïve she was when it came to lovemaking, and had been put off by it.

It was perhaps as well that they were not so busy in her office that day, because her mind was by no means on her work. It was around mid-morning, however, when, still thinking about Lyle, she was feeling warmed to remember how, put off by her naïveté though he might be, he had still called her a bewitching creature. And he had said '... a man could lose his head over you...' she thought dreamily—then realised with a start that love had certainly made her forgetful. Her love for Lyle, of being with Lyle, had made a nonsense of her, she discovered, because only then did she remember how she had planned to tell him over dinner that she was giving up what his father had so mistakenly left her. So enraptured had she been just to be with him that, while they had talked on every other subject, she had forgotten completely the most important one!

'All right with you if I have an hour off as soon as I can arrange it?' she looked over at Nadine to ask, deciding to act now, immediately, before love should again wipe her memory blank. 'I need to have a chat with Brian Rawlings.'

'Of course,' Nadine smiled. 'Our workload seems to be on the decline anyway.'

Smiling her thanks, Kelsa got on the phone to Burton and Bowett, and then to Brian Rawlings' secretary, but only to discover that Brian Rawlings was out of the office all that day. 'His diary is absolutely jam-packed on Monday, too, Miss Stevens,' the secretary began to apologise, asked what it was in connection with, and when Kelsa revealed that it was about the Hetherington estate. 'Oh, *that* Miss Stevens!' she exclaimed, and as if the name Hetherington had just opened some magical door, 'I think I can slip you in at four-thirty on Monday, if that's any good.'

'That'll be fine,' Kelsa accepted, and rang off to acquaint Nadine with the fact that she'd be leaving the office some time after four on Monday.

That done, she made every effort to be work-productive for the rest of the day, but with Lyle so much on her mind she had the utmost difficulty. When late in the afternoon a gorgeous basket arrangement of flowers was delivered to their office, to concentrate on work suddenly went from difficult to impossible.

'Somebody cares,' she murmured smilingly to Nadine, believing the flowers were for Nadine, probably from her fiancé.

'They certainly do,' Nadine smiled back, and directed the messenger over to her desk.

'For me?' Kelsa queried in astonishment, and felt herself go scarlet with surprise and emotion when, checking that the envelope was indeed addressed to Miss Kelsa Stevens, she withdrew a small card and read, 'Dare I hope you're thinking of me as much as I'm thinking of you?' It was signed 'L'. 'Oh!' she gasped, and just couldn't believe it. As much as he was thinking of her? He'd never been out of her mind! 'They're—er—from a friend,' she murmured when she caught Nadine's eye on her.

'I rather gathered that,' Nadine replied with a grin. Though when it seemed that Kelsa was not going to be more expansive she tactfully immersed herself in her work.

Kelsa was still trying to calm the excited beat of her heart some ten minutes later. *Lyle had sent her flowers*! Beautiful flowers! She didn't even know where he was—in which country—but wherever he was, he was thinking of her.

She was still shining eyed and ecstatic when, with her precious flower arrangement safe in her car, she drove herself back to her flat that evening. Lyle was thinking of her! Last night he'd promised he'd be in touch when he came back. Loving him the way she did, Kelsa fought against the danger of reading into any of his words or actions anything which might not be there. But, even as she laboured to keep her feet on the ground, she felt she could be sure, couldn't she, that to have sent flowers, to have suggested he was thinking of her *at all*, must mean that when he got in touch with her on his return it would not be on a matter of business.

Because of Lyle, because he was in her head and in her heart, and because she felt inwardly so unsettled yet did not feel ready to bump into old friends, Kelsa again decided not to go down to Drifton Edge that weekend. Not that Lyle would be getting in touch so soon—he had only just gone, for goodness' sake! No way would he be coming back yet. He'd said about a week. That would take him until about next Thursday.

She spent Saturday alternately doing a few chores and sitting staring dreamily into space, or gazing at her flower basket, which stood in pride of place in the centre of a low table.

On Sunday morning she ached to see Lyle again, and, love being a dreadful taskmaster, she was finding, she started to feel ill inside at the realisation that, even supposing Lyle did return to England around next Thursday, there was no saying that she would see him then.

Love was an appetite remover too, she discovered, for she felt not the least inclined to eat lunch. Perhaps—the dreadful thought had to be faced—Lyle would leave it a week before he made contact again.

Kelsa was still in the throes of mental uproar by the time afternoon gave way to early evening. She knew that, even while she was living in hope, cold, hard logic just had to declare that one dinner, a few kisses—be they quite a few, and of mind-blowing quality, for that matter—plus a simply gorgeous basket of flowers could in no manner constitute proof that Lyle had started to care for her a little. Then suddenly, and startlingly, someone rang her doorbell—and her thoughts got suspended in mid-air.

Even as she struggled for control, for calm, and tried to tell herself not to be so idiotic and that there was no way that Lyle was going to get back this early—and why would he make her address one of his first ports of call anyway, for goodness' sake—there was hope in her heart. Dizziness turned to hope, unrealistic hope, as on shaky legs she went to answer the door.

It was not Lyle who stood there, of course—as, if she'd any brains, Kelsa realised she should have known without getting herself into such a lather. But, as she recognised her caller as a woman she had seen once in a church and once at a solicitor's office, she knew her visitor *was* one member of the Hetherington family.

'Mrs Hetherington!' she exclaimed in surprise, as the tall, stately and stony-expressioned woman looked imperiously at her.

'If I might have a moment of your time?' Lyle's mother suggested in cultured tones.

'Yes, of course,' Kelsa remembered her manners, her thoughts flying off at a tangent. 'Won't you come in?' she invited, but no matter down which avenue her thoughts dived, she just couldn't find any answer to why his mother should be paying her a visit. 'Lyle,' she asked, her voice suddenly anxious, 'he's all right?'

Her anxiety, it seemed, was not lost on her visitor, and the woman's mouth tightened. 'The Hetherington men are *always* all right! They make a point of always *being* all right!' Mrs Hetherington replied stiffly. 'It's the women in their lives who suffer.'

Kelsa didn't like the sound of that. Though both her mother and the woman in front of her had known pain through loving Garwood Hetherington, so she could not argue the fact. However, since Lyle must be in good health with no accident having befallen him, or Mrs Hetherington would have said so, 'Please take a seat,' she invited, and wondered if she should offer Mrs Hetherington some refreshment. That thought went promptly out of her head, however, when on her way to the easy chair, her guest took an interest in the flower basket on the nearby table. And while Kelsa, regretting for a moment that because it meant so much to her she had placed Lyle's card with its intimate message in a prominent position where she could see it, Mrs Hetherington stooped over to read it, including the initial 'L'.

'It's started, then!' she stated obscurely, and as if to endorse that this was not a social call and that she would not be staying long, she went and perched on the edge of Kelsa's easy chair.

'I'm sorry?' Kelsa queried, from courtesy taking a seat too and sitting opposite the starchy woman. 'I don't under...'

'The flowers—they're obviously from Lyle.' And while Kelsa was blinking at that, she went on high-handedly, 'When my sister-in-law told me over the phone this morning that you, with my son a willing participant, went to see her last Wednesday, I knew at once what he was up to.'

Kelsa stared at her in wide-eyed surprise. 'Up to?' she repeated.

'He always was a person, right from a boy, who would go straight after what he wanted. All too plainly he's not waiting any longer than for his father to be laid to rest, his will read, before he's gone after what he's determined to have.'

'Determined to have?' Feeling stunned by this woman's aggressive attitude, Kelsa didn't need it spelling out that Lyle's mother wasn't feeling very friendly towards her. Not that she could blame her for that. But...

'You didn't think he'd meekly lie down and allow you to take what he considered to be rightfully his, did you?' Mrs Hetherington cut through her thoughts abrasively.

'Well—no,' answered Kelsa, never having thought about it, but unable to see Lyle taking anything meekly, or lying down, for that matter, regardless of what the issue was. Though, as her brain began to wake up, 'If you're talking about the money, the stocks and...'

'My son, Miss Stevens,' Edwina Hetherington butted in unceremoniously, 'regardless of what he may or may not have told you to the contrary, is prepared to fight for what he wants. Regardless of the cost, he'll go after it. It's inherent in him.'

'But he doesn't...' Kelsa might have added that Lyle didn't have to fight for anything with regard to her inheritance, because she was going to, and willingly, give up all claim to it.

She did not get the chance to finish what she'd started, however, because to shock her, and to make her gasp, as much from the content of what she said as the bluntness with which she uttered it, Mrs Hetherington began hostilely, 'Let me make this quite plain, Miss Stevens. My only concern in coming to see you is that I do *not* want you for a daughter-in-law.'

'Daughter-in-law!' Utterly astounded, Kelsa gaped.

'I do not want you to be my son's wife,' Mrs Hetherington stated in words of one syllable.

'B-but...' Kelsa spluttered, hardly believing her ears. '...Lyle hasn't asked m——'

'If I know anything at all about the Hetheringtons—and I lived with one for forty years—he will. He's got his sights set on your fortune and, like his father before him, he'll be fully prepared to marry to get it.'

'I——' Kelsa tried to interrupt.

'And, just like his father before him,' Mrs Hetherington forged ahead, 'he'll marry his heiress. Only you've no need, young woman, to wake up one morning, as I did, to the cold stark truth that not only has your husband married you for your money, but that he's acquired a mistress into the bargain! You've been forewarned, and since you don't have to marry him for *his* money you're in the happy position of being able to say no. Or, which is perhaps a better alternative, since Lyle has inherited his father's persuasive tongue, refuse to have anything more to do with him.'

Staring in amazement as this domineering woman told her the whys and wherefores, Kelsa didn't doubt from which parent Lyle had inherited his harsh straight-for-the-jugular manner which she had seen plenty of when she had first known him. But, while all that his mother had thrown at her was a lot to assimilate, a sharp feeling of unease about Lyle started to make itself felt. Especially when it occurred to her how here, in this very room, when Lyle believed her to be his sister, he had been all aggressiveness and hostility. But recalling how he had changed to being kind and considerate when he knew they were not related—had that been because he had at once realised that she was therefore—she swallowed at the thought—*marriageable*!

Suddenly it really started to get through to her what Lyle's mother was saying, and although she wanted to argue that Mrs Hetherington must have got it all most terribly wrong, still she couldn't help wondering, had she too? Feeling sick inside, all Kelsa knew for sure then was a quite frantic need to be alone. Abruptly she got to her feet. More than at any time in her life, she realised she *had* to be alone so that she could think. 'Th-thank you for coming here to—er—w-warn me, Mrs Hetherington,' she hinted, and to her relief the stony-faced woman stood up.

'I have your word...' the aristocratic woman began haughtily.

But Kelsa, while certain courtesies were inbred in her, had taken enough. And her spirit, which had been floored, suddenly asserted itself. 'I'm afraid not,' she replied politely, if firmly. She desperately wanted the woman gone.

'You already have money, so there's no need for you to marry him to get it!' Mrs Hetherington restated shortly. Kelsa did not think much of her argument, so she stayed quiet, though she could see Mrs Hetherington was far from pleased, and Kelsa could have done without her parting shot as she went to the door. 'And if you're in love with him,' she stated coldly, 'then more fool you!' With that she sailed arrogantly out, and, as the door closed after her, Kelsa collapsed on to a chair.

She was still there an hour later, and had gone through again and again every word she and Lyle had ever exchanged. And by then she had realised just exactly what a fool in love she had been.

Quite distractedly she had tried to be objective. But when she went over and over everything, there were far more incidents that led her to believe that his mother was right, and that Lyle *was* stringing her along for his own ends, than there was evidence that he genuinely liked her.

For all his mother's assertion that he would marry her to get his hands on what his father had left her, though—and Kelsa's breath caught as she recalled how much he needed that backing for his future plans—she just couldn't think he would go *that* far.

Bearing in mind how tough she had seen him on more than one occasion, she could see him perhaps planning to get engaged to her, planning to love-talk her into signing everything over to him—and then dropping her flat. But for him to actually go through with it, to the extent of marrying her—no, she couldn't see that. Though... hadn't she thought, wondered herself at one time if his father had married his mother for her money? Hadn't Mrs Hetherington said as much herself an hour ago? And oh, for mercy's sake, hadn't his aunt herself said how like his father Lyle was in his way, how set in the same mould as his father he was?

By midnight that night Kelsa, with her head spinning from thinking about it so much, had come to the sad conclusion that the Hetherington men were capable of doing *anything* for money—even to the extent of marrying for it if they had to.

Once more she disconsolately took another look at the dramatic change that there had been in Lyle's attitude to her once he had known she was not his sister.

Suddenly, with breathtaking suddenness now she came to think of it, he had gone from detesting her to wanting to get her a drink of brandy! Talk about thinking on his feet! He'd barely discovered that she was not his sister than he was making her a cup of tea!

In seconds he had changed from a man who had no time for her to a man who would *find* time for her. She had no need to look beyond the way he had taken time out of his very busy day last Wednesday to take her to see his aunt to know that.

By the time she went to bed in the early hours of Monday morning, Kelsa felt exhausted. She had been over and over everything many, many times. Had been over how Lyle had called to ask her to hang fire and not to milk the company until he could raise the finance—presumably to buy her out. But what rose most constantly to the surface in all her desperate thinking was the way he had called, believing them related, but—heavens above—the way he must have done one devil of a rapid rethink once he knew that she wasn't his sister! Kelsa put her head under the bedclothes—heaven help her, she'd been a sitting target!

She was awake at six, and her first thought was of Lyle. For about ten seconds she was certain that she had got it all totally wrong, and that Lyle's mother had most definitely got it completely wrong. For goodness' sake, it was too incredible to *be* believable! Then stark reality took over.

Stark, because Lyle had said a man could lose his head over her—but he hadn't lost his head, had he? The whole time he'd been making love to her, he must have been very clear-thinking, she now realised. Unlike her, who had then, and ever since, been totally witless—oh, how green she had been! The painful truth was that he never would lose his head over her. His taste wasn't even for blondes, for heaven's sake!

With too bright a clarity Kelsa remembered the beautiful and elegant woman he'd chosen to partner that last time she and Nadine had shared a meal with his father, and abruptly, she got out of bed.

She entered her sitting-room chased by jealousy that while Lyle had dated her once, it was not blondes he was inclined to but, given free choice, he would prefer a brunette every time.

Kelsa still found it hard to believe he would go as far as to *marry* her in order to gain control of Hetheringtons. Then suddenly she recalled something else, and as shock hit her, she felt her blood go cold. For, having gone through every word, look and gesture that had passed between her and Lyle on a one-to-one basis, her thoughts went back to last Thursday. That had been the day after Lyle had taken her to see his aunt Alicia—when Mrs Ecclestone had confirmed that she was *not* Lyle's sister, because their half-sister had died in babyhood. Lyle had stopped by her office on Thursday, she recalled again, and after a few preliminaries had asked her to have dinner with him that night. She had agreed, of course she had, and had—as he'd no doubt intended all along—been swamped by his charm over dinner. But, going back, it had been after he had invited her out that morning, when Ramsey Ford had spotted Lyle and had asked him if there was any news of his plans, that Lyle had answered, 'I'm working on it,' and had qualified, bearing in mind that he was certain then that they were not related, 'Last night I thought of one excellent way to secure the backing I need.'

Feeling stunned as she realised only then that she must be every bit as unworldly as her mother, Kelsa knew that decision time had arrived. Since she had every intention of signing everything over to Lyle anyway, whether he would or would not marry her for financial gain was not the issue. What was at stake here was her pride and how she would feel when, once Lyle was acquainted with the fact that everything was his, he would forget all about his promise, 'I'll be in touch when I get back,' and would forget too that he'd sent her flowers, forget his 'Dare I hope you're thinking of me as much as I'm thinking of you?' message, and would most likely cut her dead the next time he saw her in one of the corridors of Hetheringtons. Or worse, she suddenly realised, put into action his threat to dismiss her once he had anything to do with it. The matter—without further thought—was all at once settled for Kelsa.

She did not go to work, and at ten past nine she rang her office and having asked to speak to Nadine, began, 'Nadine...'

'You've overslept?' Nadine guessed wrongly.

'No, not that,' Kelsa quickly put her right, and having had three hours in which to decide what to say, went on hurriedly, 'Would you mind very, very much if I didn't work out the rest of my notice?'

There was a kind of stunned silence from the other end, then Nadine, to Kelsa's relief, was bringing her unflappable being to the fore. 'You sound most serious, Kelsa. Have you a problem I can help you with?'

'No problem, honestly,' Kelsa to her consternation, had to lie. 'It's just that—well, I've had the weekend to think it over, and it—er—just seems right to me. If you can manage...'

'Well, of course I can manage—or get help from elsewhere if need be, but are you sure...?'

Another sticky five minutes went by, and Kelsa felt no better than she had before when, having just terminated her employment with Hetheringtons, she at last put the phone down.

That done, she phoned the agent from whom she leased her London flat and, having determined to be back in Drifton Edge by nightfall, she arranged to give up her tenancy. Knowing that the agent would have not the smallest difficulty in re-letting it, she found him most willing to liaise with furniture removers and service people with regard to the key.

'If you'll let me have the key when you're ready, it'll be no trouble,' he assured her. 'If we happen to be closed, pop the key through the letterbox—labelled, of course,' he reminded her, just as if he had dozens of keys pushed through his letterbox after hours.

Kelsa spent a very busy morning and part of the afternoon in packing up anything transportable by car, and in reflecting how she had flirted briefly with London, got her fingers severely burned, and now, while she still had her pride, she was getting out of there.

But how badly she wanted to stay was borne out for her when, as she went to dump the flower basket which Lyle had sent her, she found she just *could not*. Her hand was actually on the handle of the basket, when it froze.

Damn him! she thought furiously, and hated him and hated her vulnerability where he was concerned. Even when she knew that those flowers were a lie, she couldn't throw the wretched things out.

She still had a few small chores to attend to when she realised that she'd better leave what she was doing if she didn't want to be late for her four-thirty appointment with Brian Rawlings.

She had meant to head for Drifton Edge straight from the solicitors, but time was her enemy, and she set off to keep her appointment knowing she would have to return to her flat.

'Come in, Miss Stevens,' Brian Rawlings smiled, shaking her hand as the secretary who had shown her in went out. 'Now, what can I do for you?'

The appointment took longer than she had anticipated, because, although she had thought there would be nothing simpler than for her to say she didn't want the legacy, Brian Rawlings seemed to want to put obstacles in the way.

'You have to be very sure,' he insisted. 'What you're thinking of giving up is...'

'I'm not thinking, Mr Rawlings,' Kelsa told him firmly, 'I'm doing it. I'm very sure, and...' not knowing much about the legal side of it, she started to panic '...and nobody can make me accept it if I don't want it!'

'But Mr Garwood Hetherington wanted you to...'

Half an hour later, having at last convinced Brian Rawlings of how adamant she was, and having given him her Drifton Edge address and phone number so he could contact her about any ensuing problems or signatures required, she left his office and drove to her flat for the last time.

Back there she finished the last of her packing and, having taken the last load down to her car, returned to the flat. After taking a last look around, she was just about to leave when her phone rang.

She went over to it and, knowing this was the last time she would answer it in this abode, picked it up. 'Hello,' she said, and nearly fainted when she heard Lyle's voice on the other end.

'Missing me?' he asked softly, and while her heart raced stupidly despite having been given an antidote of pride, everything else in Kelsa went haywire. And all she knew then was that she had to disabuse this man who held her heart of any notion that she found him in any way fantastic.

'Missing you?' she queried, and with a light laugh, 'You've only been gone five minutes!'

The silence that met her words was tangible. But his tone was even when a second or so later, Lyle queried, 'What's wrong, Kelsa?'

'Wrong?' she bounced back. 'Heavens, not a thing! Other than that I'm rushing to go out.'

'You have a *date*!' he barked.

'I—er—don't want to keep him waiting,' she explained, and promptly had an earful of the Lyle Hetherington she had first been acquainted with.

For, with lightning quickness, he roared, 'Be sure not to offer him your virginity the way you offered it to me!' Kelsa was still gasping at that when his phone slammed down.

A moment later her own fury surfaced, and she was glad of it. It was either fury or tears. The swine! How *dared* he throw that back at her! From that 'Missing me?' she gathered he was still abroad somewhere. Well, all she hoped, wherever he was—and she was growing more and more angrily certain that he was on holiday somewhere, probably with some brunette—that the sun failed to shine!

That last 'brunette' thought did nothing to restore her even temper, and Kelsa almost forgot to drop the keys off at the agent's. But, that done, the finality of her actions struck her, and by the time she pulled up on the driveway of her home at Drifton Edge, she would have loved to be angry again.

Hurting inside, knowing that, because it was the only way, she had that day severed all chance of seeing Lyle again, Kelsa drove into her garage and put the car away, deciding she would unpack everything in daylight tomorrow.

On going into her old home, she put the heating on and did a few immediate chores, then went up to bed to try to find some mental rest. Her sleep, though, was of the restless variety, and it was still dark when she got up on Tuesday morning and took a shower, then pulled on some jeans and a sweater.

Lyle, as ever, dominated her thoughts while she brushed her hair in her bedroom. Though he was ousted temporarily when, in the stillness and quiet, suddenly, unexpectedly, someone rang her doorbell.

Kelsa put down her brush, realising that Len, the milkman, must have seen her light on and was thoughtfully checking to see if she wanted a delivery. Hurriedly, so as not to hold him up on his milk round, she darted downstairs and pulled open the door—then gave a gasp of pure astonishment. Because, when she knew for a fact that she had given up all chance of seeing Lyle again, when she knew for a fact that he was still abroad somewhere—who should be standing there in the light spilling out from her hall but Lyle Hetherington!

A Lyle Hetherington who was looking anything but pleased to see her, she realised, when, having waited long enough in his opinion for her to say something if she was going to, he waited no longer. 'I trust your house guest has gone!' he snarled aggressively.

'He——' she managed, but as somehow it dawned on her that Lyle must be referring to the date she'd told him she had, 'He didn't stay the night!' she retorted, and, with her heart banging thunderously against her ribs, she stood amazed when, grim-faced, he strode forward.

'I want to talk to you,' he rapped, and before she could stop him he had pushed past her into her hall.

'Come in, why don't you!' she snapped acidly, but as he turned and favoured her with a dark look for her sarcasm, Kelsa knew he was back to being the brute of a man she had first clashed with. Without the least idea of why he was back in England, or why he was paying her a visit, all she could hope was that, whatever his reason was, she didn't end up hitting him for a second time.

CHAPTER NINE

THERE was a determined look about Lyle which Kelsa didn't much care for. But while despite the energetic pumping of her heart she had no wish to play hostess to him, since it was clear that he hadn't driven all the way to Drifton Edge—and at this time in the morning—without some purpose, she led the way into her sitting-room.

Once there, having flicked on the light, she promptly put some space between them. If they were going to have a row—and no man could incite her to anger like this man—then she did not want to be close enough to be able to physically lash out at him.

'I thought you were abroad somewhere?' she fired for openers.

'I'm going back this afternoon,' he clipped, all too plainly feeling about as friendly towards her as she was feeling towards him.

'Oh?' she murmured, and instantly killed the ridiculous notion that fleetingly surfaced that Lyle had jetted in especially to see her. 'Surely, if you've returned to collect something you'd forgotten, you should be at your home or office, not here?'

Icily he eyed her, his expression giving nothing away. No clue there whatsoever for her to pick up whether he'd been on holiday or away on business.

His icy stare, though, was making her feel uncomfortable, as if *she* was in the wrong somehow! She took her glance from him and moved to the back of the settee, as though if that was between them it would afford some protection before he got started. And he would, she knew it. She could feel it, that kind of tension in him as though, coiled and taut, he was about to have to let go—with her the target.

She did not have to wait any longer, she discovered. For, as she glanced at him again, their eyes met, and oddly then she saw his eyes weren't icy but smouldering—with fury! She couldn't miss the fact that he *was* furious either, when he challenged aggressively, 'What happened?'

'Happened?'

He threw her a dark look, and seemed ready to throttle her for trying to pretend she didn't know what he was talking about. 'The last time I saw you, you were a warm, responsive woman. A loving——'

'For heaven's sake!' she cut him off before he should go any further. 'How was I expected to be? You were a man outside my experience. A——'

'Don't you *dare* tell me you'd behave like that for any man!' he sliced in, outraged.

'I'm not telling you anything!' she flew, in fury, in panic. 'Nor,' she went on swiftly, 'do I want this conversation.' She took a shaky breath. 'You've obviously come here with some purpose, so...'

'So what happened?' he insisted shortly. 'We were getting along—well. I thought...' He broke off, as if he was unsure of how much he wanted to confide. But that was when Kelsa suddenly woke up. Grief, what was she thinking of? This man was out to lead her up a very treacherous garden path!

'Look here, Lyle,' she decided it was time she became assertive, 'I don't know what you read into my—um—hm—response the...' Oh, heavens, so much for being assertive! 'Anyhow,' she resumed hastily, 'if you've taken exception because I've dated someone else, then...'

'Did you date someone else?' he demanded sharply, and when she stared at him, the reinforcing lie refusing to leave her disloyal tongue, 'It couldn't have been much of a date if you drove down here afterwards!' he charged. In her view, he was much too smart for his own good.

'So perhaps I didn't have a date,' she shrugged, and, as the tension in her stretched, she almost blurted out that there was no need for any of this charade. No need for him to hint that it might matter in the slightest if she dated one man or a hundred other than him, because she was signing everything over to him, so he could roll up his treacherous garden path and not linger in Drifton Edge a moment longer.

But he was watching her, making her nervous, and she couldn't think straight. She began to feel confused too, unsure, so that it seemed to her then that if she wanted to come out of this with any pride, with her dignity intact, then the less she told him, the better at this stage. Brian Rawlings would, in any case, tell him all there was to be told once she'd put her signature to any document he would draw up.

At that moment, though, as Lyle stood looking more relaxed as he leant negligently against the mantelpiece he studied her, and she would dearly have loved to know what he was thinking. But his eyes were giving nothing away, though the aggressiveness had gone from his tone, and his voice was quiet as he enquired mildly, 'Why lie, Kelsa?'

'Grief—is it a hanging matter?' she challenged agitatedly.

'You're nervous!' he picked up, and she hated him for it. 'What are you nervous of?' he wanted to know.

'Look...' she exclaimed in exasperation, 'if you've got to take a plane back to wh-wherever it is you've come from to b-be back there for this afternoon, then you'd better get a move on.'

'Not before I get what I've come for,' he told her, and there was something in his tone that made Kelsa not doubt that he meant it.

Though she knew full well that what she should be asking was what indeed he had come for, nerves got to her again. And to top everything, a fear arose in her that she might, in any ensuing fight, give something of her real feelings away.

'For goodness' sake, Lyle, it's half-past six in the morning!' she began a diversionary tactic.

'And from the scrubbed look of you and the fact that you were up and dressed when I called, I'd say you've either got a most uncomfortable bed or that you're having trouble sleeping.'

'Oh, for...' She began to panic, and in that panic promptly turned her back on him to snap bluntly, 'I've had just about enough of you Hetheringtons!' And on a shaky note, 'I'd like you to go,' she told him.

She heard him move and clenched her hands at her sides when it seemed he was taking heed of her desire that he leave. Tears stung her eyes and throat, and more than anything she wanted to turn round and take a last look at him. But she wouldn't. It had to end *now*.

Suddenly, though, at the next sound she heard, alarm shot through her and her tears dried on the instant. Because while she had been listening for the sound of the door opening and closing, she heard nothing of the kind! What she did hear and see, though, was Lyle coming into her line of vision as he stepped round the settee to face her.

She opened her lips to once again tell him to leave, but no sound came. For a shrewd look had come into Lyle's eyes and, too late, she was remembering how sharp he was. How, when it came to thinking on his feet, they didn't come any faster.

'You said "Hetheringtons", plural,' he reminded her of what, in her panic, she had said without being fully aware.

'Did—I...?' She tried to pretend she had meant nothing by the plural.

'You were fond of my father, I know that for a fact, so I hardly think you meant to include him in that uncomplimentary-sounding "Hetheringtons",' he was quick to analyse. 'Nor, despite the fact that my aunt Alicia had the unhappy task of telling you that you have no sister, do I think you meant to include her.' Speechlessly Kelsa stared at him. Then, more than ever, as she saw the way his mind was working, did she want to lie to him. To say yes, she did hold it against his aunt that she'd told her what she had. But it wasn't true, and she couldn't, and Lyle was forging on. 'So that leaves only me—and——' An added alertness came to his eyes as he said softly, 'Oh, Kelsa, that's it, isn't it—my mother's been in touch with you?'

'I...' No, she wanted to tell him, but she couldn't do that either, though she knew with some desperation that she didn't want Lyle to know the truth—that his mother *had* been in touch and that was why she had left London, because to know that Lyle was only making up to her for his own ends was more than she could take. Miraculously then, though, when she was having the gravest trouble keeping her wits about her, Kelsa suddenly found an acting ability which she hadn't known she possessed, and, her tone sounding absolutely astonished, 'Why on earth would your mother want to get in touch with me?' she asked—and had to suffer Lyle's eyes steady on her, while for long moments he gave some consideration to her and, it seemed, to his reply.

Then, to her genuine astonishment, he let fall, 'I imagine for a very similar reason to the one she phoned me about at my hotel in Switzerland on Sunday.'

And Kelsa, even as it registered that he'd been in Switzerland, was unwary in her astonishment, and simply gasped, 'She phoned you after she'd been to see me Sunday evening?'

'Oh, what a little love you are!' Lyle shook her by saying—by sounding so natural when he said it.

'What?' Kelsa questioned, her heart giddy as she tried desperately not to be affected by any throwaway endearment he uttered—no matter how natural-sounding it came out.

'For the record, my mother managed to make contact with me around lunchtime on Sunday,' he told her. 'But thank you for confirming that most awful suspicion.'

'That wasn't fair!'

'What the hell is in this business?' he wanted to know, and as Kelsa sent him a resentful look for extracting from her information which she'd never been going to reveal to a soul, it was quite obvious he had his mind on business the whole time. 'Are you going to tell me why she came to see you?' he enquired, his tone mild again.

'You're so clever, you work it out!' she threw at him hostilely—and, for her sins, he promptly did.

'Plainly it has a connection with her call to me,' he began but, leaving the subject briefly, he seemed tense again, Kelsa thought, when he went on, 'If my guesswork is anywhere near accurate, I'm going to have...' He broke off, and, stretching out a hand to her arm, requested, 'Look, Kelsa, regardless of what my mother came to say, try to trust me. Trust me, and hear me out.'

'Hear you out?' she questioned, but she was just playing for time while, his touch on her arm having a weakening effect, she tried to pull herself together.

'There's a lot I have to say, but thanks to my mother's interference, in order to convince you of my sincerity I can see I shall have to go the long way round.'

'A first for you, unquestionably,' she murmured with what acid she could find, knowing for certain that he always went straight for what he wanted with no deviation.

'Possibly,' he shrugged, 'though since I've known you there have been so many firsts.'

'I'm sure,' she offered sceptically.

'My mother's done her work well, it seems,' he observed, then asked, 'Will you give me the time I need to explain one or two matters? I need to talk to you quite urgently, believe me,' he stressed, his look so sincere, so tense, that Kelsa, even though she had hardened her heart against him, could not help but thaw a little.

'Go ahead,' she offered offhandedly.

'It may take a while—shall we sit down?' he suggested.

'You'll be asking for coffee next!' she tossed in waspishly. Though because of the weakening effect of his right hand still on her arm she moved away from him, and, finding she was round at the front of the settee, she sat down. So too did Lyle. However, since it was a three-seater settee, although he was closer to her than she would have liked, he was not overcrowding her. 'You were saying?' she hinted.

'I was saying——' he took up, hesitated, and, turning so he could see her expression the whole time, 'To go back to the very beginning, I first saw you...'

'And immediately assumed I was your father's mistress.'

'Shall I tell this?' he hinted.

'Be my guest,' she shrugged. She might have been weak by agreeing to let Lyle have his say, but she had, thank goodness, been warned by his mother, and if he was leading up by some devious route to so much as mention the word 'engagement', let alone 'marriage', then was he in for a sharp answer!

'So there was I,' he resumed without waiting for further invitation, 'about to go to Australia . . .'

'You first saw me when you came back.'

'I first saw you *before* I went.'

'You did? Where?' Kelsa asked, having got over her weak moment, and not prepared to believe a word without first questioning.

'In the firm's car park.'

'I didn't see you.' She'd have remembered him, she knew that. Even without knowing who he was, she would never have forgotten the tall, sophisticated Lyle Hetherington—who could?

'I wasn't in the car park. I was in a rush, having been delayed when I called briefly, as I thought, at the office for some last-minute paperwork before leaving for Australia for a month. I was impatient to be off, couldn't wait for the lift, but as I turned to go down the stairs I caught a glimpse of you from the landing window. You were getting out of your car, and I...' He paused, seemed to need to take a steadying breath, then went on, 'I watched you walk, oh, so gracefully, across the car park, and thought you were the most beautiful woman I'd ever seen.'

Her mouth fell open, and she just stared at him. She wanted to believe him—oh, how she wanted to believe him! But Mrs Hetherington had called to see her. Had... Suddenly, though, Kelsa remembered, without remembering exactly when, but she clearly recalled thinking at one time, that she hadn't known that Lyle knew her car. But if he'd seen her getting out of it, as he'd just said, then . . .

'Er—carry on,' she invited, when it seemed as though he was waiting for some comment, some hint of encouragement, perhaps.

'I saw you, and knew I—had to know who you were.' He didn't wait any longer. 'By that time, having watched you until you were out of sight, I took off, and reached the ground floor just as you were crossing the reception area away from me. In no time, with the help of a nearby male, I'd found out that you were Kelsa Stevens, newly acquired secretary to Ian Collins in transport, and...'

'You said I was walking away from you—so presumably I was walking away from the helpful nearby male too,' Kelsa butted in, having no intention, despite Lyle's heart-stopping comment that he thought her the most beautiful woman he had ever seen, of letting him get away with anything unchallenged.

'You were,' he agreed, 'but your superb legs and lovely blonde hair are known the length and breadth of the building. There are few men at Hetheringtons who couldn't have told me who you were.'

'Oh,' murmured Kelsa, sorely needing some stiffening from somewhere. 'So you saw me, and that was that?'

'No way,' he argued. 'I was already running late, and I knew I had to get a move on if I was to catch my plane. So all I could do then was to decide that perhaps I might take a stroll around the offices of the transport section when I got back, and...'

'But in the month in between, you promptly forgot everything about it,' she inserted matter-of-factly.

'Forget you—*never*!' Lyle declared vehemently, and her heart began to race again. 'I arrived back at head office late on a Monday afternoon,' he went on, as if everything was crystal-clear in his mind. 'I knew, or thought I knew, that my father would be at his usual Monday afternoon meeting, but I'd already decided that, rather than disrupt any point they were discussing, I'd take a stroll along to the transport section.'

'You went there before you actually went to see your father?' Kelsa gasped.

'Didn't I say you were on my mind?' he responded, and while Kelsa fought hard to keep a grip on herself, he continued, 'Having found my way to Ian Collins' office, though, what did I find but no blonde head bent over a desk, but a plain if pleasant secretary. Naturally, I asked her how she was settling in.'

'Naturally,' Kelsa agreed, a shade warily. 'And naturally you asked what had happened to me?' she suggested, wondering if he was lying, why he should lie?

'I didn't want you working for any company but Hetheringtons,' he explained, 'I wanted you where I could see you, where I knew I could contact you should I want to.'

'Er—naturally,' she mumbled, her eyes showing her disbelief.

'Try to believe me,' he urged. 'I'm telling you it all, as it happened, because while I've an idea wild horses aren't going to get out of you what passed between you and my mother yesterday, I know she can be blunt to the point of cruelty if...'

'She has a son just like her!' Kelsa found some stiffening to insert coolly.

Though she was promptly deflated when Lyle accepted, 'I deserve that, and more. But, to get back to Ian Collins' office, when I suggested to his new secretary that Kelsa Stevens hadn't stayed long, she, to my amazement, told me that you hadn't left, but that you'd transferred to the chairman's office. I was still taking on board the fact that when other, longer serving secretaries more confidentially experienced had been overlooked so that you could have that prize job, when I walked back up and into reception—only to be hit sideways by another shock.'

'Ah!' Kelsa exclaimed as her brain started to work overtime and events began to slot into place. 'That was when you saw your father and me leaving—and laughing.'

'I'd never seen him look so pleased with life,' Lyle told her. 'And I was as mad as hell!'

'You followed us!'

'And damn near came into your apartment building and confronted the two of you.'

'You did?' She hadn't known that.

Lyle nodded. 'I couldn't take it in. But I realised I needed to think before I did anything.'

'You're usually pretty good at thinking on your feet,' Kelsa got in.

'This was one time when I was too absolutely staggered for that to apply,' he revealed. 'I was too upset, not only that it appeared that my father had taken leave of his senses, but that he had done so with a woman whom I...' Lyle broke off, and then, with his eyes holding hers, he quietly added, 'whom I had—fallen for.'

'*Fallen for*?' she questioned, her voice husky despite her firm intention that he should have not the smallest notion that he affected her one way or the other. 'But,' she protested, as ice-cold sanity flooded in to trample uncaringly on hope, 'you hadn't so much as even spoken to me then!'

'I know it sounds crazy, but I didn't need to. It was just—*there*!'

What? she wanted to ask. What was there? How much? How much had you fallen for me? Is it anywhere near a tenth of how much I've fallen for you? Had Edwina Hetherington not paid her a visit on Sunday, she might have done. But his mother had paid her a visit, and this was all so very much along the lines of what she had said.

So Kelsa shook her head, and from somewhere found the courage to tell him, 'I don't need this, Lyle. I want you to go.'

'You want me to go? Before I've told you everything...? Before I've...?'

'I don't want to hear any more!' she stopped him before he could go any further, and as everything in her—her love for him, the shock of his mother's visit, her flight from London last night, the shock of him being with her, here and now—all churned up inside—and peaked, 'Look here, Lyle Hetherington,' burst from her, her emotions in an uproar as she shot to her feet, 'I don't want to hear another lying word!' He was on his feet too, and fearing he might again take hold of her by her arm, she took a step away. 'Your mother told me how it would be. How...' Abruptly she stopped, suddenly aware, if she hadn't been already, that she was in danger of giving her innermost feelings away.

'Don't stop there. Tell me!' urged Lyle.

'No!'

'Is that fair?'

'Yes, it damn well is!' she retorted in panic. 'Just go!'

'And if I refuse? If I refuse to go until you've told me what misguided misconceptions my mother has put into your head? If I——'

'Oh, stop it!' cried Kelsa.

'So you'd misjudge me just because——'

'Why shouldn't I? *You* misjudged *me* enough!'

'I deserve that. Dear God, I deserve that,' he admitted. 'But——'

'But nothing!' she interrupted him hotly. 'Can't you see that I'm just not interested!' she lied—but began to falter in her decision that he must go unheard, when she actually thought she saw him lose some of his colour.

'Aren't you?' he persisted. 'Aren't you interested?' And Kelsa knew then that, be it a boardroom or wherever, Lyle Hetherington wasn't a man who gave up easily.

'No, I'm *not*!' some actress in her came out for a second showing.

'Then *tough*!' he snarled, but for all his grim tone Kelsa heard him take a long shaky breath before he went on, 'Dammit, woman. I refuse to have my life ruined just because...' He broke off, to resume, 'You may not want to hear any more, but you're going to. You may not want to tell me what went on in your conversation with my far from saintly parent on Sunday, so I'll tell you how my conversation went with her when she tracked me down on Sunday.'

'I don't...' Kelsa had been about to say that she didn't want to hear any more. But—and she knew she was being pathetic, since it was not her they were talking about, and since the discussion was therefore well away from her and her emotions—she shrugged, and offered a careless, 'I don't suppose it was anything *too* important.'

Lyle, to her surprise, took her comment with no more than a slight narrowing of his eyes, then revealed, 'It seems it was important enough for her to check straight away for your address—it's there in my father's will, a copy of which we both have.'

'You're suggesting her phone call to you triggered off her subsequent visit to me?'

'I'm certain of it,' he said. And, reaching forward, he touched her arm anyway. 'Come on, Kelsa,' he said gently, 'I know that one way and another both my mother and I have treated you very badly. But if I'm ever going to be allowed to try and make it up to you, then please forget everything about my mother's visit to you on Sunday.'

Didn't he know how much she wanted to forget about it? Didn't he know how wonderful had been that feeling that had followed on from that enchanting dinner she'd had with him, his flowers, the message that had come with them? Oh, how wonderful it would be to go back and for her to feel as she had felt before his mother's visit.

'But she did visit me,' she had to tell him woodenly.

His jaw hardened, and a determined look entered his eyes. 'I'm not going to let her spoil everything for us, Kelsa,' he growled with quiet doggedness. 'I'm just not!' And, while Kelsa was equally determined not to get excited about that 'for us', Lyle, as if considering he had pussy-footed around for quite long enough, gently but firmly propelled her nearer to him, so that the only way she found to put some distance between them was to drop down and retake her seat on the settee. Lyle followed suit, but that determined look was still on him when he resumed resolutely, 'Starting with that phone call to me in Switzerland, it seems that my dear mother, having some quite sweet and generous moments despite her tendency to be a tartar at others, rang Aunt Alicia to offer her a set of pot lids from my father's pot lid collection as a memento. In the ensuing conversation it appears Aunt Alicia told her about our visit to her last Wednesday.'

'I'm—listening,' murmured Kelsa, having nothing to challenge him with so far—but on the lookout for anything that didn't ring true.

'From there,' he took up, his solemn grey eyes fixed on her distrusting brilliantly blue ones, 'the subject of your mother came up, and, of course, you.'

'Of course,' she concurred, and didn't care that Lyle seemed to think she was being rather uncommunicative—she had no intention of being in the least helpful.

'Since it was the only time I'd ever discussed my father's affair with her, I said I was sorry for all the pain she must have been through because of it, but added that you were a lovely woman and that perhaps I might bring you to meet her.'

'You didn't!' gasped Kelsa, even if it could be said that they had already 'met' at the solicitors' office, shaken out of her uncommunicative attitude by what he had just said, and appalled for his mother's sake.

She was doubly shaken by his reply, though. For, first giving her a long serious look, 'I have plans for you and me, Kelsa,' he stated forthrightly. 'There's no way I'm going to hide you away as if you, and my feelings for you, don't exist.'

'Lyle, oh, Lyle!' she exclaimed, her heart ready to explode, her soul in torment. If only she could believe him! She wanted to believe him, oh, so much did she want to believe him—but she had been warned.

'It's all right,' he soothed, a warm hand coming out to take hold of her agitated right hand. 'There's nothing to be nervous about,' he read the way she was feeling. 'Never again will I do anything to harm or hurt you. Just try to trust me for a little while longer—I'll prove to you I'm sincere, I swear it!'

'I...' she gulped, seriously needing help from somewhere. She found it by latching on to the substance of what he had been saying before he'd mentioned his feelings for her. 'W-what did your mother say—when you—um—suggested you might take me to meet her?' she asked.

'I'm afraid she isn't very receptive at the moment. It's understandable, given the circumstances, I suppose.'

'Which means that she said, "Over my dead body", or something similar,' Kelsa guessed.

'It was more a "Why on earth should you want to bring the daughter of your father's mistress to see me?" sort of comment. Though, ever an astute lady, before I could tell her she was demanding to know, "You haven't lost your head over her, have you?" My reply,' he went on, 'must have spurred her to decide she would stop this before it went any further. It's my regret, my dear,' he breathed, his eyes fixed on hers, 'that, instead of talking it over thoroughly with me, she opted to pay you a visit instead.'

By that time Kelsa didn't know where she was any more. Lyle was looking at her with such a warm light in his eyes that she could hardly think straight.

'What was—your reply?' she just had to ask.

'The truth,' he answered. 'I'd thought about you constantly while I was away. I planned and thought, and hoped, and by that phone call on Sunday I knew that, if my hopes and plans came off, she'd have to know anyhow, and again hopefully, before very much longer.'

'I see,' Kelsa murmured, but she was just playing with words while she worked up the courage to ask, 'The truth?'

'The truth, my very dear Kelsa,' he answered tenderly, 'is that I'm heart and soul in love with you.'

'Oh, L-Lyle,' she stammered agitatedly, 'I don't know what to believe any more!'

'Oh, sweet love, my mother really put the boot in, didn't she? But forget about her,' he urged. 'Just think of you and me, us, and what you know—what you feel. Hold on to the fact that I love you, so much, and have done ever since that day I first saw you.'

'Love at first sight!' she whispered.

'I'm my father's son in that respect, it seems.' Lyle smiled gently at her. 'According to my aunt, he took one look at your mother and was lost. While I, dear love, took one look at you and, even while my hard head said it just doesn't happen like that, my heart knew, quite simply just knew, that you were the one for me.'

'No!' she denied.

'But yes,' he insisted. 'Love it is, and love it was, and for the first time ever I hated my job, which meant I had to speed off to Australia, when what I most desperately wanted to do was to speed after you.'

'Oh—Lyle!' Kelsa whispered shakily, everything in her urging her to trust, as he'd asked, to believe, but...

'I'll make you believe me,' he vowed. 'I'll take you with me to see my mother. I'll get her to repeat the telephone conversation we had. She'll tell you, without any prompting from me, how, never having confessed anything of the kind before, I told her of my deep and abiding love for you.'

'Y-you'd do that—for me?'

'We'll go now,' he stated without fuss, and seemed about to help her up from the settee when she stopped him.

'I'm—you're rushing me! I'm not ready yet!' she said quickly. 'I-I need time t-to assimilate—to-to sort my thoughts out. I need to go over...'

'We have all the time in the world,' Lyle came in gently. 'If there's anything you want to know, to go over again, we'll take the time. Just believe me when I say that there's a love in me for you that just won't go away. A love that's been giving me hell, affects my eating and sleeping—and don't mention jealousy, because that viperous, swinish, gut-picking green-eyed nagging monster jumps up on my shoulder at the smallest cause!'

'You've been jealous!'

'Jealous? I've been awash with jealousy. So stewed up with it when I thought the "something personal" my father wanted to discuss with me might be a disclosure that he was setting up home with you, that I determined not to give him the opportunity.'

'When what he really wanted to confide was his belief that I was his daughter!' Kelsa stared at Lyle wide-eyed.

'And I was too worked up to give him the chance, so instead, to my regret, I came to you with my vile accusations and temper.'

'You weren't to know,' Kelsa excused him softly, and was smiling at him as he was tenderly smiling at her, when her own jealous demon reared its ugly head and her smile swiftly departed.

'What's wrong?' Lyle wanted to know at once.

Now, Kelsa realised, was not the time to be bashful. 'What would be wrong?' she challenged. 'You were so much in love with me that you'd barely been back from Australia a week when you were dating a lovely-looking brunette!'

'I love it! You were jealous too!' Lyle exclaimed, with such an engaging grin that Kelsa could have hit him.

'Not in the slightest!' she disowned.

'Would it help if I confessed that I've known Willa Jameson for donkey's years and that, in a ridiculous and unsuccessful attempt to tell myself that I didn't give a damn about any female named Kelsa Stevens, I phoned Willa and asked her out?'

'Purely in a platonic way, I'm sure,' Kelsa brought out her best offhand manner to retort.

'Sweet darling,' Lyle grinned, 'you can bank on it. What I'd forgotten, though,' he went on, his face sobering, 'was that Willa's mother and my mother are friends.'

'Oh!' Kelsa exclaimed, her brain racing into action. 'You looked so furious in that restaurant, I felt sure you were going to come over and give both your father and me a tongue-lashing.'

'It was a close call,' he admitted. 'But just in time I realised that I didn't want it getting around Willa's mother's circle of friends—my mother's circle too—that my father was having an affair. That was the night,' Lyle went on seriously 'that, with my mother away on a cruise, I determined that, regardless of my own feelings, I'd have everything put to rights by the time she came back. I decided I'd go and see my father at the weekend, but, in the meantime...'

'In the meantime, you came to see me at my flat—and offered to buy me off,' Kelsa recalled.

'Don't remind me! You can have no idea of the feelings of remorse I've endured. Insulting you the way I did. Frightening you half to death when I was so angrily determined to make you pay for hitting me. Yet...' he paused, then owned, 'To this day I still don't know where I found the control when, wanting you like crazy, I walked away that night.'

'Yes, well,' Kelsa gulped, and remembering her warm reaction to Lyle's lovemaking, looked hastily for a change of subject, remembered sadly, 'But you didn't get to see your father that weekend, because he died.'

'So much has come to light since,' Lyle inserted quietly. 'My father wanted you there at the hospital, but didn't have the strength to tell me he thought you were my sister.'

'He'd know you'd find out, though,' Kelsa murmured softly. 'My name alone was bound to mean something to your mother and your aunt. And if they both decided to stay quiet, then there was also that birth certificate just waiting to be found.'

'Ye gods, don't remind me of that birth certificate!' Lyle stated gruffly. 'I fairly reeled out of that office when I found it.'

Kelsa remembered that day. Lyle had walked past her without a word or so much as a glance in her direction. 'Ottilie Miller mentioned that you went out for a few hours first thing that morning,' she recalled.

'I needed to clear my head, to try and think straight.'

'It was a—bad time for you?'

'Bad? I felt I'd been kicked in the gut when I came across that certificate!' he replied feelingly.

'You weren't—pleased, to know I hadn't been having an affair with your father?' she queried hesitantly.

'*Pleased*!' he exclaimed. 'How the hell could I be pleased? I wanted to marry you—and you were my *sister*!'

Kelsa's breath escaped on a rush. 'You wanted to marry me?' she cried, her eyes huge in her face.

'Did—do,' he said sharply. 'Will, if I have my way. Why in thunder do you think I've been explaining all I've explained, if it isn't to get you to see that you're the only woman for me—that you're my love, my life?'

'Oh, Lyle,' Kelsa whispered shakily.

'Are you going to tell me you love me?' he added.

'No,' she said, but even as the word left her she was aware that he already knew how she felt about him.

'All right, sweet love,' he agreed gently. 'So what else can I tell you? Shall I tell you that before I knew you couldn't be having an affair with my father, I'd seen you proud as you'd refused my offer of a lift. I'd wondered then whether, though all the evidence was there, I'd got it wrong. But only to find out the very next day when my father's will was read that he'd left you half the business—confirmation there, in anyone's book, that something had been going on between you. What else can I tell you?' he asked. 'That, even while wanting you out of the company, I couldn't take steps to dismiss you, because to do so would mean I shouldn't have you where I could see you each working day.' Kelsa was still feeling shaken by that, when he went on, 'Should I tell you how, when I called at your flat the night before I found that certificate, how with your beauty, your flashing eyes, not to mention your sincerity, I wanted so much to believe you?'

'You said you'd see what you could do,' Kelsa remembered. 'It seemed as though you might be prepared to believe me—and,' she confessed shyly, 'I was happy.'

'Were you, love?' he breathed softly, and Kelsa felt her backbone melt.

But, 'Mmm,' was as far as she dared go.

'Oh, sweetheart, you really are putting me through it!' Lyle murmured. But manfully he held himself in check. 'You know, of course, that I'm aching to hold you in my arms?' he asked, and, receiving no reply, 'Just like the way I wanted to hold you, to cradle you, when you looked so shattered to learn that my father had known your mother.'

'Honestly?'

He nodded. 'But how could I? I was feeling vulnerable and still finding it hard to believe you weren't my half-sister. It made me afraid to take you in my arms, even if only to comfort you. Then you confessed how you'd sometimes been lonely, and I was so moved that I just had to kiss your brow—but again I felt I had to back away.'

'And I,' Kelsa had to own, 'knew, while I so dearly wanted to find my sister, that I didn't want you for a brother.'

'I'm hoping with all I have, dear, dear Kelsa,' he breathed, 'that that feeling stems from the same reason as my own.'

'You said, just before we went to see your aunt, that finding out more concerned you too.'

'Most definitely it did,' he declared firmly. 'I needed all evidence that you were *not* my sister documented, verbally confirmed if possible, so that one day soon—hopefully soon—I could ask you to marry me.'

'And—er...' Kelsa tried to think clearly, but with all that Lyle was saying so confusing, she knew she wasn't doing too well. 'So—um—once your aunt had confirmed it, you—um—asked me out to dinner.'

'And a wonderful evening it was for me too,' he agreed. 'Oh, you were so enchanting that night, my dear little love,' he breathed, which was not the smallest aid to her need to get herself back together. 'Is it any wonder that, when we returned to your place and I took you in my arms, I almost lost my head?'

'But you didn't,' she whispered chokily.

'I came close,' he admitted. 'I broke out in a cold sweat when I discovered that you truly are a virgin—and, it suddenly struck me, couldn't be taking any precautions, and that like your mother before you, you were at risk of being made pregnant by a Hetherington.'

'Oh!' she exclaimed in surprise, such a thing never having dawned on her.

'I couldn't risk that. I didn't want anything to cause you worry and unhappiness—didn't want anything to hurt you. But in those moments of being so fired up emotionally, all I could see was that I had to think of you, not me.'

'Oh, my dear!' Kelsa breathed, and knew then that Lyle was a very different man from his father. Garwood Hetherington had made love to her mother without thought to the consequences. Lyle—and she believed him—loved her with a love that wanted only the best for her. 'S-so you left, and the next day you sent me flowers at the office.'

'I couldn't send them to your flat in case you were coming down here straight from the office that night. I wanted you to know I was thinking of you that weekend,' he smiled.

'Your mother saw them—and your note. She—um—asked me to give her my word that I wouldn't marry you.'

'The *devil* she did!' he exploded. 'What did you say? Did you give her your word?' he asked tensely.

'I—er—told her I was afraid not.'

'You darling! You love!' Lyle exclaimed joyously, and gathered her in his arms, and Kelsa, in the warmth of his embrace, was entirely without resistance. 'So at last we get to the point of why she called on you,' he murmured, his face against hers, appearing to want every last shred of anything that might disturb her cleared away.

'Not quite, actually,' Kelsa had to tell him—if she was dreaming, she never wanted to wake up.

'Don't stop there,' he urged, his arms a haven around her as he moved his head so he could see into her eyes.

'Well,' she said on a shaky breath, 'it was your mother's opinion...' Suddenly she halted. As dreadful as Mrs Hetherington had been, it somehow didn't seem right, after what she must have been through, to blacken her name.

'Come on, darling,' pressed Lyle. And as if knowing how she was feeling, 'Right now, it's just you and I who matter. Later, if it's your wish, I'll work out some way of reconciling my mother. But for now, think only of us, and how much you mean to me, and how I don't want to be in ignorance of the smallest issue that might later rear up to cause upset.'

'You're right, of course,' she answered, and when with his secure arm about her shoulders he gave her an encouraging squeeze. 'Mrs Hetherington seemed to think there was little you wouldn't do to get your hands on the inheritance your father left me—and that included m-marrying me to get it.' There, it was out, and looking at Lyle, Kelsa saw his forehead lift in surprise.

'Oh, my dear, dear darling!' he breathed. 'And you believed her?'

'Everything seemed to fit,' she explained shakily, 'The way your attitude changed the moment you knew for sure that I was—um—marriageable.'

'Oh, sweet love, I've explained that. It was because, after our visit to my aunt when I knew for sure we weren't related, only then could I begin to pay any warmer attention to you—begin my courtship. Oh, hell,' he groaned, 'it fits either way, doesn't it?' Then, on a decisive note, 'You'll just have to come with me to see my mother. We'll confront her together, and make her tell you every word of my conversation with her over the telephone.'

'I don't think that will be necessary,' Kelsa murmured.

'What do you mean by that?' he asked sharply. 'You're surely not turning me down? You're not letting her——?'

'What I mean,' Kelsa cut in with a smile, 'is that I trust you. Which in turn means that there's no need for us to go and confront any...'

'You trust me!' he echoed. 'Oh, you sweetheart,' he murmured, and just had to lean forward and place a tender kiss on her warm and parted lips. 'My dear Kelsa,' he said, a huskiness in his throat, 'you trust me, despite how it must have looked when I sent you flowers, when

I... No wonder you pretended you'd got a date when I rang last night!'

'I'm sorry about that,' she apologised, her eyes shining with her love for him, her heart beating an enchanting rhythm. Lyle loved her—oh, it was so fantastic! 'Though...'

'What, my love? I don't want you to keep anything hidden from me.'

'It's nothing really, just that, after your mother's call on me, I had a dreadful time of it.' Lyle's tender kiss on the side of her face was all the balm she needed, and she went on, 'I had to believe her—that you would—well, at least get engaged to me, especially when I remembered how, only on Thursday morning, the day after we'd visited your aunt, I heard you tell Ramsey Ford how you'd thought the previous evening of an excellent way to secure the backing you needed.'

'You thought I meant—*you*?' he asked, his astonishment so real that Kelsa could in no way doubt it. 'Hell take it!' he exclaimed. 'I never for a moment...' He broke off, but then went on warmly, 'How I wish I'd left that damned door open! If I had, you'd have heard me outlining to Ramsey the plan I was working on to put before some Swiss bankers whom I'd been setting up meetings with some minutes earlier. The backing I need from them, my love,' he revealed with a loving look, 'seems virtually certain.'

'Oh, Lyle!' she sighed, and then, as a thought came to her, 'You planned to buy me out, didn't you?'

'That was my plan,' he agreed. 'I'm good for quite a bit in my own right, so I thought, independent of the company, to...'

'But you don't have to buy me out!' she couldn't wait to tell him. 'I'm making everything your father left me over to you—I've already started the ball rolling,' she smiled—and a moment later was left staring at him, thunderstruck.

'I know,' he smiled, 'and...'

'You *know*!' she gasped.

'Brian Rawlings told me when I...'

'But—but...'

'What is it, love?' he asked gently as she seemed to be having difficulty in stringing a sentence together.

'But if you already know—knew that, before you came here, then it confirms that you aren't—don't intend to marry me for th-that fortune!' she stammered hurriedly.

'You do realise, you darling woman, that *you've* just agreed to marry *me*, don't you?' Lyle questioned with a wide and warm smile that was wonderful to see. Then, not waiting for her shy reply, 'With or without that damned fortune, Kelsa Stevens,' he said severely, 'you belong to me. Are you *now* going to tell me you...'

'Just a minute,' she cut in. 'You said Brian Rawlings told you, but it was only late yesterday afternoon that I went to see him!'

'So he said,' Lyle told her, and explained, 'I rang him at his home some time after a most unsatisfactory telephone call to you.'

'From Switzerland,' she documented, feeling rather shamefaced.

'From Switzerland,' he agreed. 'In my fury, my jealousy—how *dare* you date anybody but me!—I knew I had to try and concentrate on something else or go insane. I went back to my desk and saw I needed legal advice on something that might have been a problem. I rang and discussed it with Brian. But, having soon dealt with the problem, Brian, to my astonishment, then told me how you'd been to see him with regard to giving up your inheritance, and had emphasised that you'd like him to complete his paperwork as quickly as he could.'

'Oh, Lyle!' Kelsa breathed softly. She had trusted him, and here was the reward for that trust! He *did* love her and *did* want to marry her, and it had nothing whatsoever to do with what his father had left her—because he'd known in advance that all that was going to be his anyway.

'I like the way you say my name,' he murmured, and gently drew her to him. Tenderly he kissed her, then drew back, to reveal, 'Little darling, I went from astonishment to feeling absolutely poleaxed when Brian said you'd given up your job, were giving up your flat, and were moving back to Drifton Edge.'

'So that's how you knew I'd be here?'

'I didn't, not then. At first I was so dumbfounded that it took me a while to straighten things out. But I couldn't rest, and knew that I would never be able to rest until I'd seen you. In next to no time I'd arranged my flight and rearranged my schedule for today.'

'Oh, you haven't slept!' she cried, seeing for herself the lines of tiredness around his eyes.

'Who could sleep when my head was so full of questions? Why had you done what you had? Why, when from the way you'd spoken on the phone I'd have said you couldn't stand the sight of me—why were you intending to make everything over to me?'

'Your—um—mother isn't interested in the firm,' Kelsa thought to mention. 'And I don't feel I have any real right to it.'

'I don't know about that,' Lyle smiled. 'Though when you're my wife it will all be yours anyway. But, to go on, I was so much in love with you and my head was in such a spin about you—then suddenly I began to hope.'

'Hope?'

'Hope that you might have some feeling for me other than hatred.'

'How did I give myself away? I thought I was most careful.'

'Wretched woman,' he berated her lovingly, 'you didn't. That's to say, only when I pieced together individual incidents did they start to come together as a whole.'

'I believe I once accused you of being *too* clever,' she laughed.

'One does one's best,' he grinned.

'So tell me,' she prompted.

'There'd been a chemistry between us from the first,' he obliged. 'You'd responded to me that awful night when I started to force myself on you,' he recalled.

'I've realised since that there had to be something special about you for me—even then,' Kelsa owned, and was kissed for her reward.

'Then I recalled how last Thursday we'd dined together, and how enchanting it had been and how you'd seemed to be feeling something of the same too—I would swear I hadn't been mistaken. I remembered how, when that night we'd kissed and embraced, you'd looked at me with loving eyes. How, when I knew full well that you just aren't promiscuous—forgive me, my dear—you'd have been mine and would have freely given yourself to me. So I just had to stop and wonder: was my love, who looked so like her mother, like her in other respects too and would give freely of herself—but *only when love was there*? Were you, in fact, dared I hope, in love with me? By the time my plane landed I didn't know where the hell I was, and I tore off to your flat...'

'You went to my flat first?'

Lyle nodded. 'And even though your car wasn't standing in its usual place, I went and leant on your doorbell for an age before deciding to try your Drifton Edge address.'

'Brian Rawlings told you my address?' Kelsa queried.

'I was in such a state, I forgot to ask him. But luckily,' he grinned, 'I've got a mind that files away things that might be important, and I remembered this address from your birth certificate.'

Lovingly, Kelsa looked at him. 'And drove here straight away.'

'There was no chance I was going to sleep, that was for sure,' he assured her, and continued, 'Pinning my hopes on the fact that your house might still be the house you were born in, or that Drifton Edge was small enough for someone to tell me where you lived—I was too churned up to think of looking in the obvious place, the telephone book—I put my foot down, got here, saw your upstairs light on—and for the first time in my life was attacked by nerves.'

'Oh, my dear,' she whispered, 'was that why you were such a brute when you first arrived?'

'From that wonderful-sounding "my dear", can I take it you've forgiven me?' he asked, and when she smiled went on, 'It started to get better once we got talking. Once we did, I began to catch a glimpse here and there of the girl I'd dined with last Thursday. When you told me how my mother had visited you last Sunday, I began to feel sure I must be right and that you did feel something for me.'

'Because, after her visit, I gave up my job and bolted?' Kelsa enquired.

'From what I've learned of you, sweet love, remembering our battles, I'd say you aren't the running away type.'

'I'm not,' she agreed.

'Not unless something has happened to you—emotionally—which you fear might be so much more crucifying if you stay and face it out.'

'You *are* clever!' Kelsa smiled.

'So put me out of my suspense, and tell a man who's nowhere near as clever as you imagine in this world of wanting a beautiful woman with the most fantastic blue eyes for a wife—do you, or do you not, love me? Are you, or are you not, in love with me?'

'Yes, to both,' she whispered. 'I love you, Lyle, and I am in love with you.'

A flame of joy lit his eyes. 'And will marry me?' he asked.

'And will marry you,' she agreed.

'My angel,' he breathed, 'I adore you!' He was pulling her closer to him when, looking down into her eyes, he stated throatily, 'I can't bear to be parted from you any longer, my love. Will you come to Switzerland with me this afternoon?'

'Oh, Lyle!' she squealed. 'Me?'

'Well? Will you?'

Kelsa took a big gulp of breath. Then, 'Yes,' she agreed, and as their lips met and her heart raced she knew she couldn't bear to be parted from him either.